W9-DBL-260

UPPER EAST SIDE

Also by Bernard F. Conners

CRUISING WITH KATE

DANCEHALL

TAILSPIN

THE HAMPTON SISTERS

DON'T EMBARRASS THE BUREAU

UPPER EAST SIDE
» GIRL «

Bernard F. Conners

British American Publishing
Latham, New York

Published by British American Publishing, Ltd.
19 British American Boulevard
Latham, New York 12110

Library of Congress Cataloging-in-Publication Data

Names: Conners, Bernard F., author.
Title: Upper East Side Girl / Bernard F. Conners.
Description: Latham, NY : British American Publishing, [2016]
Identifiers: LCCN 2016029662 I ISBN 9780945167587 (hardcover)
Subjects: LCSH: Manhattan (New York, N.Y.)–Fiction. I GSAFD: Love stories.
Classification: LCC PS3553.O512 U67 2016 I DDC 813/.54–dc23
LC record available at https://lccn.loc.gov/2016029662

ISBN 978-0-945167-58-7

Cover Photo: Image used under license from Shutterstock.com
Elevator Photo, p. 27: Courtesy of Extreme Exclusive, www.eex.eu
Central Park Photo, pp. 124–125: ©iStock.com/dolphinphoto

Printed in the United States of America

First Edition

Book design by Toelke Associates

"For CCC"

She was a Phantom of delight
When first she gleamed upon my sight;
A lovely Apparition, sent
To be a moment's ornament . . .
. . . A dancing Shape, an Image gay,
To haunt, to startle, and way-lay.

William Wordsworth

CHAPTER 1

It was a lovely summer morning, a heavenly day, when saints
and sinners gathered at St. Patrick's Cathedral for a morning of preaching and prayer. Parker Livingstone was walk-
ing past the church on Fifth Avenue when the thought flashed
through his mind that perhaps he should stop and light a candle
for his mother, who had passed away several years before. It was a
fleeting notion, as were most of his spiritual inclinations.

Although Parker had been briefly exposed to Catholic religion
as a child by his father—an occasional churchgoer—any real interest had long since diminished with his father's death years before.
His mother, a professed Episcopalian, had done little to foster spiritual interest, her own church attendance confined to little more
than her three weddings of which there had been two in rather
light-footed succession following his father's death. A striking

blonde, whose soulful blue eyes conveyed a misleading sense of divinity, she had wasted little time taking advantage of her God-given appearance. Alas, her final church involvement was a hastily conceived requiem following her disappearance from aboard a yacht in the Adriatic during the last of her honeymoons. Although a puzzling denouement to a vivacious career, her passing could only be attributed to the fathomless sea.

It had been a devastating loss for her only child, Parker, who adored his glamorous mother. Despite counseling as a youngster, he had difficulty accepting her death, and even with professional help there remained ongoing dreams and periods of depression. But his loss was not without a measure of good fortune, for he found himself the beneficiary of his mother's enterprising nuptials with a modest inheritance.

Parker continued his walk up Fifth Avenue, spiritual feelings fading. What was a candle worth, anyway? Little more than a flickering on life's stage quickly snuffed out by time, as was everything. He was often gripped by the impermanence of things, regarding time as an incomprehensible force that rendered life illusory and meaningless. But he had been warned about the dangers of being consumed by such notions. He was aware of great philosophers who had found the prolonged study of time to be a gateway to lunacy.

It was Sunday morning, an idle day for Parker, free from the strains of his job at the Candida Jones Literary Agency. Under his arm he carried a hard copy of a book he was writing, a roman à clef that reflected much of the dilemma confronting first-time novelists. One of the more troubling issues in his manuscript was a character who had taken on a life of her own, and who was now out of control. What had been devised as a thinly disguised cameo role for his boss, Candida Jones, had gotten out of hand: the benign personality he'd intended had blossomed into a flaming vexatious character. It would do little for his aspirations at the agency should Candida ever see the manuscript. Candida was not one to be pilloried without thunderous retribution.

At 59th Street he entered Central Park intending to work on his novel. Once in the park he breathed deeply, taking in the restful signs of spring that replaced the tumultuous sounds of city living. With the exception of an occasional distant blast of a cranky horn from beyond the park, it was altogether peaceful, a fitting place for an aspiring author. He proceeded to a bench where he often sat, near an exit across from his apartment at 822 Fifth Avenue, a place where he had sometimes rested with his mother during earlier years.

He had been sitting for several minutes when he noticed a young woman approaching in the distance. There was something about her carriage, a distinctive carefree gait that caught his attention, the leisurely saunter of someone who seemed supremely confident and happy with life. As she neared he was struck by her beauty. In her early twenties, she was tall and slender with blonde hair, her head tilted back slightly with a touch of imperiousness, or perhaps nonchalance. She was wearing a navy blue suit, high heels, cloche hat, white gloves, and carrying a small pocketbook which she swung casually as she walked. Although perfectly tailored, her garb struck him at first as a bit unusual. But it was Sunday, he thought. Perhaps she was coming from church.

As she passed where he sat she cast a brief look in his direction. Her eyes held his for an instant, her face softened, her lips curved ever so slightly. Was it a smile? Had she thought she knew him? For a second he was transfixed. Had he seen her face before somewhere? In a movie? A dream? Although the briefest of glances it was unforgettable, almost haunting. But it must be his imagination. This was Central Park. Beautiful women didn't smile at unknowns in Central Park. Tragically, all of the predators were not confined to the nearby zoo.

He watched the woman closely as she passed. Almost as quickly as she appeared, she was gone, disappearing into the heavy foliage beyond a bend in the path.

For a moment he was gripped by a feeling of regret. The encounter had lasted only a few seconds but it had been more than a brief exchange of looks. Yet all that remained was a vague feeling of fascination and curiosity that he felt would never be satisfied.

Finding it difficult to concentrate, he rose from the bench and walked to the exit a short distance away that faced his apartment on Fifth Avenue. Here, he paused. Although Fifth Avenue was a one-way street, he glanced in both directions. Parker Livingstone took nothing for granted in the tangled no-man's land of Manhattan traffic.

❖ ❖ ❖

CHAPTER 2

The apartment Parker had inherited from his mother's estate was in a cooperative building in Lenox Hill on the Upper East Side of Manhattan across from the Central Park Zoo. Designed by a renowned architect at the turn of the century, it was regarded as one of the most attractive and fashionable buildings on Fifth Avenue. Its residents included some of the more prominent families in America, and the move for Parker from his pedestrian quarters in lower Manhattan, although daunting, promised entrée to important social circles.

The building had its own dining room, unusual for Manhattan, which was splendid for entertaining. Cocktails and dinner parties were common, and the dining room staff helped occupants prepare for their guests.

Although at first intimidated by his new neighbors, after a few months Parker gained more confidence, and developed a casual relationship with some of the residents. The design and ambiance of the building contributed to spontaneous interactions with other occupants, particularly on the elevator. Overcoming a shyness that had troubled him since childhood, he sometimes exchanged pleasantries with riders, and even on occasion might introduce himself as a new resident. Indeed, the novel he was writing included some gentle satirical passages that dealt with his social elevation in the building by means of the elevator.

Beyond the doormen at the front entrance of the building was a large room decorated with oil paintings, flowers, and Jacobean furniture. An alcove on the side housed a large desk where two mature, attractive women were seated. In addition to greeting visitors, they acted as rather sniffish concierges for the occupants. Past the foyer were elevators and the entrance to the private dining room.

Parker's smile elicited a restrained greeting from the women when he passed through the lobby on the way to his apartment. A new and relatively younger resident, he sensed the ladies felt that he had yet to gain his stripes in the lofty air of 822 Fifth Avenue. As he waited for the elevator he glanced toward the dining room. It appeared empty, save for one elderly lady who was emerging through the door. Quickly he moved back to avoid being noticed.

"Hello, Mr. Livingstone."

Too late! Mrs. Feddyplace had seen him.

Mrs. Feddyplace was an octogenarian whose apartment adjoined Parker's on the 23rd floor. Theirs were the only units on the floor, and were joined by a tastefully decorated foyer into which one stepped after leaving the elevator. During previous visits with his mother at her apartment, she sometimes remonstrated about Mrs. Feddyplace. "She's a dear soul, but she has some dementia. When her staff isn't there she constantly rings my doorbell wanting to talk. She doesn't hear well, and turns her TV up so loud it shakes the walls." Parker's inevitable contacts with the woman were wearying and, although always courteous, he rarely lingered.

"Are you going up, Mr. Livingstone?" said the woman, moving forward and positioning herself between him and the elevator. "I'll ride up with you. I haven't seen you recently. Have you been away?"

"Hi, Mrs. Feddyplace. Pleasure to see you. Lovely day. . . ." Parker was tempted to avoid the elevator ride if possible. It could lead to all manner of things. An invitation to tea . . . to lunch . . . discussions about his mother. . . . Maybe he should indicate that he'd left something out front. . . . No, he'd tried that before, and she'd told him she'd hold the elevator. No, there was no way out. He mustn't be rude. His day was going to include a ride on the elevator with Mrs. Feddyplace.

It was a tiresome trip to the 23rd floor. Tedious conversations about her daughter . . . her grandchildren . . . the dining room. . . . And a constant refrain that things "aren't like they used to be." It seemed in Mrs. Feddyplace's fading world that nothing was like it used to be, including Mrs. Feddyplace. A few weeks before she had shown him an album of herself as a lovely young woman: picture after picture of the International Debutante Ball at the Waldorf Astoria in New York City where young ladies of prominent families, wearing white gowns and kid gloves, were presented in a coming-out affair to high society. An emotion had gripped him as he gazed at the old photos, an odd sense of having been at the event himself.

As he looked at the young photographs of the elderly woman, he was consumed by thoughts of the relentless, unsparing nature of time. The pictures brought memories of earlier days with his mother when he stood beside her as she sat gazing into the mirror at her dressing table. Although she was strikingly beautiful, disturbing signs of aging had asserted their presence in the form of tiny wrinkles near her eyes and mouth. She'd spent hours before the mirror with ointments, desperate to forestall the inevitable. Her misgivings were not lost on her only child. He recalled once when his childhood efforts to comfort her had brought from her a hug and a tear. "It's all right, Mommy," he'd said. "I'll still love you when you're old. But Mommy, if God can do anything, why would he ever let pretty girls grow old?"

CHAPTER 3

Candida Jones had done it the hard way. A part-time waitress who had made it through City College with a BA degree, she had realized her ambition as a New York literary agent. In her early thirties, tall with black hair, smoldering dark eyes, a body of the martial arts black belt variety with temperament to match, she could prove attractive to men who wanted adventure in their lives.

Starting as an intern at a small magazine, she had a modicum of knowledge of publishing, and when the opportunity presented itself at a friend's struggling literary agency, she had not hesitated. The purchase of the agency had been accomplished through existing cash flow, long-term payables, and a modest bank loan. A few best sellers had followed and within a few years she'd moved her agency from her Greenwich Village apartment to a respectable suite on West 51st Street.

Parker, a tall, sandy-haired, reasonably handsome young man in his mid-twenties, responded to her ad for an assistant, and she had not hesitated. A graduate of Williams College who had taken some courses at the Iowa Writers' Workshop, and had low to moderate salary expectations, he seemed a good choice. What Parker had not anticipated was the woman's involving him in nonbusiness activities such as lunches, dinners, and invitations to social events. Since she did not take rejection well, their association had presented all manner of problems for her employee.

Parker did his best to conceal his feelings. He had limited interest in many of her activities. Having inherited his mother's skills in establishing harmonious associations, however, he found the first few months with Candida to be relatively easy. But with time her commanding approach to their relationship became increasingly difficult.

"What do you mean, you're tied up?" from Candida. "We always have lunch on Wednesday."

It was Wednesday morning at the Candida Jones Agency. (Candida had found it useful to drop her family name, Rosenblatt, and adopt the name of her former friend from whom she'd made the purchase.)

"But what about Julie over at Macmillan?" eased Parker, sensing impending problems with his boss. "I told her about the Gordon novel and—"

"That bipolar bitch!" snapped Candida. "Don't waste your time. She'll be gone in six months."

Candida's blunt and often obscene language was jarring to Parker, particularly when she was not inclined to negotiate, which was most of the time.

"Okay, okay," he replied quickly. "Lunch it is. Four Seasons okay?"

"Yeah, sure. Oh, a woman called to reschedule your appointment for next week."

"Thanks," said Parker quickly, uneasily. "Twelve okay with you?"

"Fine." Then without a beat she added, "Why are you going to the doctor?"

Parker was surprised. How would she know about his doctor—a matter most people considered personal. "What do you mean?" he asked, confused, uncertain how to respond. "What are you talking about?"

"Oh, c'mon. I could tell when she called last month. Women who work at doctors' offices all sound the same. I could tell immediately. Nothing wrong with seeing a doctor."

Parker struggled. He certainly had no desire to discuss his medical issues with her. Still, Candida as his employer had access to personal records, including his health insurance. Maybe in some way she had discovered something that roused her interest. Once curious, Candida was as tenacious as a hound dog.

"Oh, it's nothing really," said Parker quietly. "A personal matter," he added with finality.

"Okay," she said quickly. It was apparent Candida saw little value in continuing the conversation. "I just thought I could be helpful. Okay, call Julian at the Four Seasons."

"Thanks," said Parker, resignedly. "I appreciate your confidence," he added dourly.

Parker retreated to his desk where he sat down, concerned. He knew staff in doctors' offices were discreet when calling about matters concerning patients but even someone without Candida's extraordinary powers of perception would sense something in an overly guarded call. The very last person he would want to know about any medical issues was Candida. And knowing Candida, she wouldn't be satisfied until she had all the facts, as well as discovering any disparaging information about the doctor. It was just Candida's nature—curious about everything, especially other people's personal lives.

As he sat thinking about how to deal with his boss, his thoughts returned to the girl he had seen in the park. Although days had passed since that Sunday morning, she continued to occupy his mind. It was more than just her beauty and manner; it was the lingering look she had given him, almost as though she knew him. It was strange. Indeed, mystifying.

❖ ❖ ❖

CHAPTER 4

Several weeks passed and it was late summer before Parker had completed his plans for the first draft of his novel. Candida had become an increasingly volatile and unlikable person in his book. His efforts to put distance between the character in his novel and the real Candida were unsuccessful. At one point she was described as "a Mafioso in drag." There was no question. It was all Candida.

One evening as he was leaving the office with the manuscript under his arm, Candida asked, "What's that?"

"What's what?" replied Parker, with a touch of panic.

"That! The thing you're carrying under your arm!" repeated Candida, raising her voice a few decibels, now thoroughly curious.

"Oh, this," said Parker, doing his best to sound casual and deflect her interest. "Just something from the slush pile. Thought

I'd look at it tonight."

It was the flimsiest of answers; given he made no secret of his lack of interest in reading unsolicited manuscripts—a chore with which he was stuck.

The hard dark eyes fastened on him told him he was in trouble, heavy trouble. He moved toward the door, expecting the chilling words, "Let's see it!"

"Gotta go," he said quickly, cutting off additional queries. He was out the door in a flash, feeling Candida's stare burning into his back.

It was a warm midsummer evening as he wove his way through crowded sidewalks up Fifth Avenue. He was plagued by thoughts of the consequences of the near miss with his boss. Her dominating inclinations and their relationship were becoming increasingly burdensome—an imminent unavoidable disaster, insofar as his job was concerned.

At the entrance to Central Park he hesitated. It was getting late and shadows had lengthened. Not too soon for an early evening mugging. Instinctively, he transferred his cash to a back pocket of his trousers, thereby minimizing the loss should he be required to hand over his wallet.

As he approached the bench where he often sat, his thoughts again turned to the beautiful young woman he had seen a short time before. She had found her way into his novel, as did many disparate things in a roman á clef. She was a passing character at this point, but who could tell. . . .

He'd been resting on the bench for only a few minutes when

he noticed a disheveled-looking figure approaching. In the dim light he was uncertain, but as the person grew closer he suspected it was a homeless man. Anticipating he would be approached, Parker looked away to avoid eye contact. It appeared the person was going to pass without speaking, when suddenly he stopped.

"Sorry to bother you," the man said in a hoarse voice. "Could you spare a few dollars? I haven't eaten all day."

Parker stared at him for a moment, struck by his wretched appearance. He was elderly, with a heavy beard, weary features, carrying what appeared to be a three-ring binder, and looked indeed as though he were experiencing troubled times. But what caught Parker's attention in particular was the man's voice; it was not that of a down-and-out vagrant, but rather the type of voice Parker might hear in the elevator from a resident in his building.

Parker hesitated, then drew his wallet from his pocket and handed the man a twenty dollar bill, the smallest he had. "Here you are," he said. "I hope this helps a little."

"Thank you, son," said the man. "That's very generous. Thank you very much."

"You're welcome. I wish it could be more." Parker continued to look at the man curiously. There was a certain elegance about him, his overall manner, the tilt of his jaw, that did not fit in with Parker's idea of a homeless man. Also, he thought it somewhat unusual for a vagrant to be in that area. Most of the homeless he saw were near Times Square or other highly populated places. Impulsively he said, "Do you spend much time here in the park?"

The man emitted a short laugh, which was interrupted by an ominous, grating cough. "You mean why am I not over on the West Side with all the other bums? Well, I usually am. Every now and then I come up here, though. I used to have a girlfriend in this area. Actually, I used to sit with her right there where you are. I come up now and then and think about her. Never met anyone like her. Beautiful person. When I lost her I lost everything. Thank you, son," he said, turning away abruptly. "Nice of you to help me out."

Parker gazed at the man shuffling off into the lengthening shadows rippling through the leaves of a grove of trees. As he watched the elderly form dissolve into the darkness, he was struck by the fleeting nature of time and reversals of fortune.

Bundles of dark gray images began to form in the foliage. A light midsummer breeze floated through the treetops causing the images to come alive. Parker shifted on the bench uneasily. It was time to leave.

CHAPTER 5

Candida was rarely late for appointments, and she expected the same from her employees. Parker was therefore troubled to realize that given the chaotic nature of Manhattan traffic, he was going to be twenty minutes late. Just the week before he had rattled her nerves when late for a meeting with an important author.

Consequently, he was becoming increasingly frustrated as he stood in the foyer outside his apartment, looking up at the dial above the elevator. Although Parker had harbored a moderate uneasiness toward elevators since childhood, working in Manhattan had forced him to overcome such fears. The dial showed the car was on the second floor, a full twenty floors below, and seemed to be moving with the speed of a sundial.

The stairs were an option. But twenty-two floors! Desperate, he glanced toward the old elevator in the hall nearby that had serviced the building in its earlier years. It had been abandoned long since and, in fact, bore a prominent sign above its door:

NOTICE
ELEVATOR OUT OF SERVICE
DO NOT USE

Out of sheer frustration, Parker walked to the elevator and pushed its down button. No response. He pushed the button again, and then pounded on the door. Suddenly, the clunking, low grumbling sound of something that shouldn't have been disturbed came from behind the door. Within minutes it opened and he was standing before a very old but beautiful antique elevator.

Impressed, Parker warily stepped into the car. The elevator was larger and infinitely more decorous than the one for daily use. Soft cherry paneled walls covered the interior and the floor was covered with a time-worn Persian rug. Suspended from the ceiling was a decorative chandelier which, although inoperative, gave the appearance of a tiny ballroom. A small light fixture with a chain seemed to be an expedient source of light. Prominent on the rear wall was a large mirror and, beneath the mirror, a cushioned settee. The impression was that of a small Victorian anteroom.

Recovering, Parker pulled the light cord to illuminate the interior, and then, impulsively, pushed the bottom floor button.

Again came the reluctant rumble as the car descended. The ride was longer than he'd anticipated and he was having regrets—particularly with the unnerving shakes and vibrations that accompanied the descent—when the car jolted to a stop. Suddenly, the light went out and he was in total blackness. Alarmed, he groped for the light cord, but was unable to find it. As he ran his fingers along the panel of elevator buttons hoping to open the door, slowly, almost imperceptively, he sensed a presence. A vague chill settled over him. Yes, he was certain now. There was something right next to him in the elevator. He sensed a creeping sensation as though a soft hand were stroking him lightly on the neck. Anxiously, he pushed what felt like the lowest button on the panel. The door opened and he discovered that he'd been delivered to what appeared to be a cold basement. Hesitating, he stepped into the dark room, looking for a way to the main floor. As he proceeded cautiously through the dim light, again he felt a presence next to him that seemed to be drawing him farther back into the cellar. With each step came waves of fear and nausea that he sometimes experienced during stressful situations. As he instinctively resisted the feeling, he saw a stairwell on the far wall. Quickly, he moved across the dank passageway and mounted the steps to the ground floor.

Regrettably, from Parker's standpoint, the door leading from the cellar was in view of the occupants at the front desk. Parker's emergence from the cellar where residents rarely visited would be of curious interest to the older ladies who bore the sentinel responsibilities.

"Good morning, ladies," Parker greeted them with a weak smile, masking his anxieties.

"Good morning," murmured the ladies, their inquisitive eyes boring in on him.

Once outside, waiting for a cab, Parker reflected on the odd feeling he had experienced in the building. In the light of day, he rationalized that it had been little more than his imagination. It was not unusual for him to sense such strange emotions—a common affliction among writers, he reasoned. Still, he could not put out of his mind the bizarre feeling that he had not been alone in the elevator or cellar.

His late arrival elicited little more from Candida than a glance at her watch and a slight frown. The fact that they were having lunch at the 21 Club with one of their authors that day may have contributed to her forbearance.

"Make sure Bruce doesn't put us back there in Siberia," Candida snapped.

Parker was on the phone with Bruce Turner, manager of 21, making their reservation. "Siberia" was the most remote part of the dining room at 21, and Candida had made it clear that if she was being gouged four hundred bucks for lunch, there was no way she was going to be remote about it. Bruce was the handsome urbane maître d' who had borne the displeasure of Candida's seating arrangement in the past. They would not be in "Siberia."

They arrived at the restaurant, a short walk from their office, and Candida proceeded to work the room, greeting people she knew, as well as those who hadn't the foggiest notion who she was (a practice despised by Parker who, when introduced at all, was that of a minion in her organization).

It was after two by the time they finished lunch. Their guest had left when Candida finally asked the question Parker had dreaded. Would he like to have a drink that night . . . maybe dinner? Although he'd practiced an answer to the question many times, it was now stuck in his larynx.

"I'm sorry," he muttered, averting his eyes. "What did you say?"

"I think you should have your ears tested," exclaimed Candida, black steel in her pupils. "You heard me! I asked if you wanted to have a drink tonight. You know, a *simple* drink!" she added sardonically.

"Oh, sure," Parker responded, now in recovery mode. "It's just that I'd planned on going to a movie tonight with—"

"Good, we'll go to a movie," she interjected, cutting him off.

". . . my cousin," finished Parker hopelessly. It made no difference. They were going to the movies. She hadn't even heard the "cousin" part of his excuse. It was just as well. There was no cousin.

Dinner and a movie that night with Candida was a long evening. A drink at her place afterwards was narrowly avoided because of his claim of acid reflux, an excuse that was partly true. For him, a night with Candida could be as stomach-wrenching as a tryout with the Flying Wallendas.

❖ ❖ ❖

CHAPTER 6

The thumping beat from Mrs. Feddyplace's apartment was unusual. Often the television was turned up to its max, and the fact that it was on the wall next to Parker's bedroom was a constant source of annoyance. But this was something different. He knew Mrs. Feddyplace was not into hip-hop so she couldn't be listening to what he heard come pounding from her apartment. She'd probably gone out and left the radio on. Ordinarily he could have tolerated the music, but it was Saturday, a day off from the office, and he'd intended to work on his novel. Hip-hop was the last thing he wanted in his ears, particularly when he was attempting to reorganize troubling digressive themes in his book.

Finally, he put the manuscript aside and walked to a front window that offered a broad view of Central Park and its surroundings. To the left was a large pond that served as a skating rink during winter months, while directly ahead was the wide expanse of the Central Park Zoo. From his window he could see the polar bears cavorting in their man-made rocky environment of pools and caves. At the moment, one bear was having a difficult time attempting to extricate a large blue beach ball from one of the pools. He sympathized with the bear's persistent efforts in what seemed a hopeless cause. Turning from the window, he walked to the manuscript on his bed. Although overcast, it was a reasonably pleasant day. Perhaps he'd take his book over to his favorite bench in the park.

He was in the hallway preparing to push the elevator button when the old abandoned elevator came to mind. Then, an idea. The elevator was never used. It had been quiet in there. There was a comfortable bench. What better place to do some writing? Why not, he thought, moving toward the car. Once again he noted the inscription above the door:

NOTICE

ELEVATOR OUT OF SERVICE

DO NOT USE

After pausing for a moment, reflecting on the sign, he pushed the button. There was no response, but when he pushed the button again there came the familiar low grumbling and rattling sounds that indicated it was on its way. Within a few minutes it came to a bumping stop. Gingerly at first, he stepped inside and pulled the small chain attached to the electric light. The bulb flashed on, illuminating the interior. Perfect, he thought. After glancing at the settee, he returned to his apartment where he obtained an additional cushion from a sofa in his living room. Within seconds, manuscript in hand, he was comfortably ensconced on the settee in the privacy of the elevator.

It was quiet as a crypt, and he was taking satisfaction from his decision when he heard a slight sound. At first, it was little more than a soft tinkle such as one might hear in a church ceremony, but it was soon followed by a more insistent ring that demanded attention. Only then did he hear the clunking, growling response from the elevator and the feeling of moving upward. And the trip was not one of short duration, but up, up, up.

He was wondering if it would ever reach its destination, when it finally stopped. After a pause, it groaned upward a few more feet and then came to a grinding halt—the sound of a machine that had been pushed to its very limits. Where in the world was he? Someone must have summoned the elevator. He was pondering what he should do when the door began to creak open. And then, lo! To his astonishment, before him stood the beautiful young woman he had seen days before in Central Park. She appeared as startled as he, but was the first to recover.

"Gosh!" she exclaimed, wide-eyed. "You're the first person I've ever seen here—I mean in this elevator. Do you work in the building?"

"No, no," replied Parker, standing quickly, striving for

equanimity. "I was just doing some writing," he stammered, displaying his manuscript.

"Yes, I see," said the girl. "You're not living in the elevator, are you?" she said with a facetious smile.

"I live on the 23rd floor," Parker said, shifting uncomfortably. "I just thought it was quiet here. I didn't think, you know, that anyone used this elevator."

"We're not supposed to," she said. "It's really not safe. If the elevator got stuck you could spend some time in here. It has an alarm, but they may not hear it." She spoke in a somewhat aloof, confident tone with a trace of British accent. Parker listened quietly, charmed by her exquisite features and a manner that was both reserved and friendly. She seemed relaxed after her initial surprise, almost indifferent to his presence.

"Do you use this elevator often?" he asked, attempting to make conversation.

"Sure, sometimes when the other one's busy. Not supposed to. No one uses it. You're the first person I've ever seen here. But it takes forever getting the regular elevator up here when it's in use."

"Uh, you're on this floor?" asked Parker. "What floor is this anyway? It doesn't show on the buttons there."

"You're on the roof," she said, smiling. "The penthouse."

When she laughed or smiled, which was often, he noticed a dimple in her right cheek. The striking blue eyes and vivacious smile reminded him of his mother.

"Well, we best go," she said, turning to the elevator buttons.

"I wonder if they could use an operator for this hickey," she said, waggishly. "Maybe I could do a little moonlighting. What floor did you say, sir?" she asked, mimickingly.

"23rd," he replied. "I'm on the 23rd."

As they traveled down to Parker's floor he tried anxiously to continue the conversation, their unexpected meeting having left him at a loss for words. "Didn't I see you recently in the park?" he said. "One Sunday morning? I thought you might be coming from church."

"Church?" she laughed. "You may have seen a different person. But I do spend lots of time in the park. Jogging. Have to be careful, though. Strange people in the park. Particularly at night. Can be a dangerous place."

"Yes, it really is," he agreed. "But probably no more dangerous than Manhattan traffic. The park's probably less hazardous than a New York cab."

As they neared his floor, he tried to think of some way to introduce himself without it seeming awkward or presumptuous. Such an enchanting woman would be forever fending off aggressive males.

They came to a jolting stop on the 23rd floor. As he picked up his pillow from the bench and prepared to leave the car, he turned toward her and then, almost impulsively, said, "By the way, permit me to introduce myself. I'm Parker Livingstone."

"Hi, Parker. I'm Sarah. Sarah from the roof," she added with a dismissive laugh.

Was it that she didn't want to tell him her last name? he

wondered. . . . As the elevator door began to close, she held it briefly, as if inclined to delay her departure. "It was a pleasure meeting you, Parker. Perhaps we'll meet again here on the elevator." She offered a slight wink, followed by an easy smile that tingled to his toes.

CHAPTER 7

Life settled into boring routine at the Candida Jones Literary Agency on West 51st Street. But thanks to one of Parker's mid-list authors, who received a splendid review in the *New York Times Book Review,* his fortunes at the agency had improved. Candida's interest in her employee continued unabated, and the added revenue derived by Parker's author had not gone unnoticed. It was with a measure of good will, therefore, that she had given him a raise and assured him he had a bright future in the agency, maybe even a sort of junior partnership. Although appreciative, Parker was a trifle ambivalent about anything that would lead to a closer relationship with his aggressive employer.

Several days had passed and there had been no sign of the dazzling girl in the elevator. He had thought about her

constantly, hoping for another chance encounter in the building, perhaps in the elevator or dining room, but to no avail.
He toyed with the thought of making a query at the front desk,
but it would have been awkward. As a relative newcomer in the
building, he continued to receive a polite but reserved reception from the ladies out front. From his mother he had learned
that the modus vivendi of the aloof residents in the building
was maintaining strict privacy. Besides, even if he knew more
about her it probably wouldn't help. It seemed doubtful that he
would have a ghost of a chance to form any sort of relationship
with a radiantly beautiful young woman he had encountered
in an elevator. Hopes of meeting her often made him linger in
the dining room, and even prompted him to take the old elevator on two occasions. It would be nice to see her, if only for a
few minutes. Maybe he'd have the opportunity to tell her more
about why he'd been in the old elevator; to explain about Mrs.
Feddyplace and the need for a writer to be free of distractions.
She had to have thought it bizarre for him to be secluded in
such a strange place.

The opportunity came when least expected. It was a Saturday
morning in August, a trifle overcast with a promise of rain over-
head in the rustling leaves. He was seated in the park on his favorite bench with his head buried in a manuscript assigned to him by
Candida, unaware of a figure approaching from down the path.

"Aren't you the chap who hangs out in the old elevator?"
came a light feminine voice.

Startled, he looked up, and found himself looking into blue

eyes. "Sarah . . . why, Sarah . . . how nice to see you," he stammered, closing the manuscript and rising, struggling to cope with the unexpected.

"I thought it was you," she said, continuing to move on. "Don't let me interrupt you."

"No, no, you're not interrupting," he said anxiously. "Ah, would you have a second? I just wanted to explain—you know—that elevator situation. I hope I didn't frighten you."

"Not at all. Weren't you reading a book or something?" she said, brushing aside her blonde hair. Dressed in navy blue exercise clothes and white sneakers, she radiated an exuberance that he found captivating. "As you can see, I'm doing my road work."

"Yes, I see," Parker agreed. "Would you have a minute?" He gestured toward the bench. "I'd like to talk to you for just a second."

She hesitated briefly, then said, "Of course. But only for a minute. I'm running a bit late on my workout." She dropped onto the bench beside him. "So, tell me about your work," she said, expressing interest in the manuscript he was holding. "Something you're writing?"

"Oh, this isn't mine," he said. "I work for a literary agency so I read lots of manuscripts. Say . . . I hope I didn't frighten you in the elevator. You must have thought it weird for me to be sitting in there working on my book. You see, my neighbor Mrs. Feddyplace is hard of hearing, and sometimes she turns her television up pretty loud. It's a bit distracting. Since that old elevator is out of service I thought it might be a quiet place to write."

"How interesting. You're writing a book? What's it about?"

"It's a novel, about time," Parker said, shifting uneasily. "Nothing special, really. It has a number of different themes. It's kind of hard to explain." He sensed his time with her would be limited. He certainly shouldn't waste it talking about his novel. "It's about book publishing and theoretical physics," he added, hoping the esoteric nature of the theme would discourage her from pursuing the subject.

"Oh, I was just reading about that in the paper. Do you write about quantum physics?"

"No. No, not really. I took some physics courses in college and . . . say, uh . . . Sarah, I'm Parker Livingstone," he said, hoping she would volunteer her last name.

"It's nice to see you again, Parker," she said. "I'm Sarah Holloway. Tell me more about your book. I'm interested in things like that."

Despite his efforts to learn more about her, she persisted with questions about his novel, displaying a surprising knowledge about theoretical physics. So transfixed by her charm and intellect was he that he was unprepared when she suddenly got up.

"I'd better get on with my running," she said, starting to move.

"Pleasure to see you again, Sarah," he said, rising from the bench. "I'm sure we'll meet again . . . in the building or here in the park." His mind racing, he struggled for some way to make a more definite connection. Dare he ask for a date? But how could he? He hardly knew her. She might think him terribly brash. It could be embarrassing. But she seemed to like him, and he might not have another chance. Then, sensing an opportunity about to be lost, he added impetuously, "Would you care to have lunch sometime?"

She paused as though weighing her answer. Emboldened by the opening, he struggled to think of a plan she would find convenient and acceptable.

"Tomorrow's supposed to be a nice day. They have box lunches to take out from our dining room," he said, surprised by his own boldness. "I sometimes have lunch here. I could get a couple of box lunches and meet you right here in the park . . . that way you wouldn't have to travel anywhere or get gussied up. . . . Twelve o'clock?" he added with a weak smile.

She regarded him quietly for a moment with cool, unnerving eyes, as though scrolling through important dates elsewhere. He was preparing himself for her regrets when suddenly she smiled brightly and said, "Twelve o'clock? Here? Why not!" Her forthright response was stated with assurance as though the issue had been settled. "Twelve it is!" she added, patting him on the shoulder.

Flashing a radiant smile, she was gone beyond a bend in the path, disappearing as mysteriously as she had appeared.

CHAPTER 8

Tension mounted in apartment 23A at 822 Fifth Avenue. It had begun with Parker in bed first opening his eyes to the bursting realization that today was the day. A day that he would have lunch with the most stunning person he had ever met. It was too early in the mating game to say that he was actually in love. Only three brief meetings? How could it happen? But love defies rationalization. It may sneak up on one surreptitiously over time, or come with the speed and impact of a fast-moving freight train. It has its own ways. What was undeniable was that he was infatuated with the girl. Her beauty, her style, her obvious intelligence, her carefree laugh, the self-assured way she had patted him on the shoulder. . . . Never had he been so taken with anyone. There had been other girls. He realized that women found him attractive. Candida, for example.

There were times he sensed she had more than an employee relationship in mind.

But now, it was Sunday, and in a matter of moments he would be with the girl who had completely overwhelmed him. But the tension increased. It had started with the weather report on television: the forecast was rain starting early afternoon. What if it came earlier? A box lunch . . . on a park bench . . . in the rain! Because of the forecast, would she even show up?

Slowly, he rolled from his bed and walked to a closet where he stood appraising his clothes. He should go for casual, he thought. Perhaps a jacket would be overdressed in the park. Maybe just a sweater. On the other hand, Candida had seen fit to comment on his new navy blue blazer. It wasn't too warm. Probably that would be best. The blazer, a light blue button-down shirt, and his blue and white saddle shoes. . . . But after a glance through a window came the sobering realization that he might well end up in a raincoat.

He was at the dining room by eleven to pick up the box lunches: two chicken salad sandwiches, a small salad, and some potato chips. In one hand he had a bag containing two paper cups and a bottle of white wine he had been saving for a special occasion. It was barely eleven thirty as he eyed the graying sky and entered the park. By twelve, much to his dismay, he felt the first few raindrops.

Rising from the bench, he walked to the shelter of a nearby tree. Soon, there was a steady drizzle. It was hopeless. It seemed pointless to wait. Yet, he was reluctant to leave. Maybe she'd appear. Raincoat and umbrella. Unlikely. It was approaching one o'clock when, gripped in disappointment, he finally gave up. Carrying the lunches and bottle of wine, he walked to the exit, paused to turn up his collar, and crossed the street to his building.

"Wretched day," offered the doorman.

Little did he know, thought Parker, immersed in despair. He was tempted to ask him if he had seen Sarah, but a man emerging from the building nodded cordially, momentarily distracting him. "Morning, sir," he said to the gentleman, continuing into the building toward the elevator.

He was about to push the elevator button when a voice came from the hall leading to the dining room. "Hi, Parker."

Startled, he looked down the darkened hallway. "Over here . . . in the elevator," continued the voice.

Turning, he moved quickly into the hall and there on the far wall standing in the open door of the old elevator was Sarah.

"I saw you crossing the street," she beamed. "C'mon, get in."

The old floorboards groaned disapprovingly as he stepped into the elevator. "Well, this is a pleasant surprise. Not a good day for our lunch," he said, shrugging. "I'd given up on you."

"I was here waiting," she said. "I wasn't sure about our lunch with the rain. I was watching and saw you come out of the park. I thought you'd be drenched."

"Oh, that's right. You must look right into the zoo from your place, just like I do." Sensing an awkward moment, and anxious to prolong their meeting, he said, "I have the lunch right here.

Why don't we go into the dining room?"

"Oh, it might be too late now," she said, glancing at her watch. "It's going for one o'clock. I have to be somewhere at two. Maybe we could just eat here quickly."

"You mean here?" he said, puzzled. "In the elevator?"

"Why not?" she said, crinkling her blue eyes. "It's a cozy little spot, right?" Without waiting for an answer she took the lunch from under his arm and pushed the button closing the elevator. "So, what do we have here?" she said, opening the bag.

Delighted by her take-charge manner, Parker quickly succumbed. He would have lunched out on the curb had she desired. "How about some wine?" He withdrew the bottle from the bag, dropping one of the paper cups in the process. Bending down to retrieve it he sat down, his back against the mirror on the wall. "We might just as well be comfortable, right?"

She was quick to join him and seemingly happy with the paper cup of wine he offered her. "Bottoms up," she said, reaching out to him exuberantly.

"Yes, bottoms up," responded Parker, smiling and raising his cup.

"Tell me more about the book you're writing," she said as they settled down for lunch. "You started to explain your theme in the park yesterday. It deals with publishing and time, right?"

"Yes, the story deals with the abstract nature of time. The temporal nature of events. The protagonist thinks of time as an incomprehensible force . . . that it renders life meaningless. For him, events lack reality because of their ephemeral character.

You know, their impermanence. His philosophy causes him to do all manner of things and, too late, he realizes such thoughts lead to madness. There," he added with a smile, "that should take care of my novel."

"To the contrary, I think it's interesting. And you mentioned it has some romance as well. I'd like to hear more about it." She sounded sincere, unlike the few other people who had commented about his book.

Stretching her legs out, she balanced the box lunch on her lap. She was dressed casually in a white blouse and tan skirt with matching white bobby socks that disappeared into tan and white saddle oxfords. His eyes were fixed on her long tawny legs when she appeared to notice and said, "Everything okay?"

"Oh, yes," he said quickly. "I was just noticing your tan. Have you been to the beach?"

"East Hampton," she replied. "I'm out there a bit. You go to the Hamptons much?"

"Sometimes. My boss has a place in East Hampton. I get invited on occasion," he said with an unintentional wince.

"Does he invite you out much?" she asked. "You don't act as though—"

"It's not a he, it's a she. No, she's nice," he said, not elaborating. Better things to talk about than Candida.

They discussed the Hamptons as they dined. Yes, she stayed at the Maidstone Club. Yes, she liked grass tennis courts, and she often went to the beach. He shifted, his shoulder leaning slightly against hers. She didn't seem to mind. He found their closeness in the quarters exhilarating. As they continued with their small talk, he was thinking of an appropriate way to initiate a future date, when Sarah moved to get up.

"Well, I should be moving along," she said, patting his hand in an affectionate manner as she stood up and pushed the elevator button. "We were rained out, but it was fun."

As he climbed to his feet, the elevator trundled upwards finally coming to a worn-out clunking halt at his floor. He was standing very near her, and possibly emboldened by the wine, he said, "How about a *real* date? This could be the start of a neighborly thing."

She laughed slightly, her face close to his as the door opened and he stepped from the elevator. "Sure, we'll see. I love being with you, Parker. Very much, actually." Then, peering at him closely, she said, "We've got a little chicken salad on our face. There," she added, brushing his cheek with her fingers. "All gone. We're friends now, right?" A final smile, half teasing, half affection, and she was gone.

CHAPTER 9

A social invitation from Candida could never be treated lightly. And this one, an invitation to her place in East Hampton for the weekend, had bordered on a command. Parker's only excuse for declining such overtures that could ever withstand a withering response from Candida was his health. Candida was a borderline hypochondriac, and claiming he had a severe sore throat was his best chance. The possibility of catching the summer flu was a real stopper for Candida.

"Oh, Jesus! Not another sore throat!" It was not going well with Candida now that he'd mentioned his condition.

"Yeah, aching all over," he added, not very convincingly.

"Well, take a couple of aspirin." Candida was not giving up easily. "I told Meaghan you were coming. I planned on working on that Kogan manuscript with the two of you."

Meaghan O'Reilly was a young employee who, having started as an intern at the agency, was now working as a close personal assistant to Candida. Parker suspected Meaghan was no happier than he with spending the weekend with Candida. "Last time out there all I did was run errands," she'd confided to Parker. "Hardly ever got to the beach."

"Go to bed early tonight," was Candida's icy response to his impending flu. "You'll feel better in the morning. It sounds like one of those one-day things. You have to take better care of yourself."

"Sure, I can take the Jitney out later tomorrow if I feel better," he said referring to the bus service to the Hamptons.

Parker's plans were quite different. An entire weekend of close quarters with Candida could have unpredictable results. But things would be slowing down in the Hamptons. Only a few weekends left, summer had begun to fade, and Hamptonites were now anxious to button down seasonal relationships. His thoughts were on Sarah continuously, and he often stopped at the park bench on the way home in the evenings, hoping to run into her. A chance encounter was his only possibility. She must have men constantly pestering her for dates. He'd already suggested another meeting, and she'd answered with a noncommittal, "We'll see." It seemed to him that her response made it clear that any future engagements would be at her discretion. But she'd said she loved being with him. Still, he had to be discreet. It would be hard to recover from an outright rejection.

He had taken the old elevator a few times, but chances of another meeting there seemed remote. Also, the way it groaned and rattled inspired little confidence. What if he got stuck between floors? How would he explain it to the management? The notice above the door clearly stated it was out of service and not to be used. And what if no one rescued him? Still, a weekend in the elevator might be better than the alternative with Candida.

On Friday morning, with the weekend looming, Parker elected to call in sick. He waited until after nine, hoping Meaghan would answer the phone. If Candida answered it would be a challenge. He practiced his "sick" voice just in case, and then made the call.

"Good morning, Candida Jones Agency." Ahh, it was Meaghan.

"Morning, Meaghan," he said, trying to make his voice hoarse. "This is—"

"I know who it is, you phony!" snapped Meaghan. "And you can forget that fake voice. You're no sicker than I am."

It was apparent Meaghan had heard about his "sickness," and was not happy about dealing with Candida all weekend by herself. Parker stifled a laugh. He could never con Meaghan. A few years younger than he was, she was a sharp New Yorker, who somehow managed to control her ebullient personality around Candida. Pretty, with a lovely smile and cute figure, Meaghan and her quick wit were more than a match for Parker. He sensed she was fond of him and, although he thought her a bit coarse, he found her attractive.

"I'm really sick," maintained Parker. "I ache all—"

"Candida's gonna be real pissed, you know," said Meaghan, ignoring him. "She told me last night that if you didn't come, she's gonna call you all day to make sure you're in bed. It might be easier for you to forget that flu crap and just come with us. She'll call you every—"

"So, she calls. I might have to go out to the doctor," he said plaintively. "Man, you women are so uncaring—"

"Parker, you know Candida," Meaghan interrupted. "She'll call your doctor. I'm telling you, you better get your ass outta that bed right now, and get in here. You may be okay now, but I'm warning you, you're gonna be one really sick dude by the time Candida gets done with you."

Parker remained quiet as reality set in. Candida had probably prepped Meaghan for his call. "Okay, okay. Boy, you guys are tough. I'll be there in a little while. And just so you know, Meaghan," he muttered. "I *am* sick and I hope you both catch it. I do have a tickle in my throat."

"Good career move," said Meaghan. "Better the tickle than strangled!"

◆ ◆ ◆

CHAPTER 10

A weekend in East Hampton was not to be sneezed at. Particularly after Candida's admonishment to "get rid of that fake cold fast!"

Parker was quick to comply: he'd made a remarkable recovery. Now, as he sat squeezed into the back of Candida's sky blue convertible, hair blowing in the wind, he was reasonably comfortable, having reconciled himself to the trip. It would be over quickly, he thought. Same lunches, same parties, same people, all frantically chasing quixotic weekend dreams.

"Remember, I don't want to get involved with Gus Ambrose," Candida warned, glancing in the rearview mirror from behind the steering wheel. "He's driving me crazy with that manuscript. He took the mother. Now he's gonna have to live with it."

Parker mumbled his acquiescence, but his thoughts were

elsewhere. His eyes were on Meaghan, whom he knew was petrified driving with Candida.

"She has no idea where she's going," Meaghan often complained. "She thinks she's Danica at NASCAR. It's just a question of time before she kills us all. I wish they'd revoke her license."

But at the moment, Parker was not concerned with the speed of their vehicle. His thoughts were racy, but they were not on NASCAR. He'd seen pictures of Meaghan at the shore in her bikini and, while he sometimes questioned her literary acumen, there was no question at all about her physical attributes. They were there in abundance for all to see, and Meaghan did little to conceal the view. While dealing with Candida over the weekend would be challenging, thoughts of strolling the beach with Meaghan were ameliorating.

Candida's "villa on the shore," as she referred to it, was not exactly on the shore, but a good city block from the beach. Located on Potato Ridge Row, her so-called "villa" had been a source of mild concern to its neighbors because of its general unkempt appearance. While not an outright wreck, the name bestowed by Candida, "Shady Gardens," was somewhat appropriate.

It was following one of the late evening parties that the inhabitants at Shady Gardens returned to their "villa," all three inebriated, particularly Candida, who collapsed on her bed and passed out. It was apparent she was gone for the night.

"I think she's done," said Parker with relief. "How about a drink?"

"A drink? Good grief, are you crazy?" said Meaghan. "I'm

plastered! And so are you."

"How about a walk on the beach?" persisted Parker. "Safe, no driving. Sober us up."

"Listen, buddy. I've had about ten margaritas. The only *safe* place for me right now is bed . . . alone!" she added with finality.

"Okay, fine," said Parker with a trace of annoyance. "I do think you have a rather unpleasant way of jumping to conclusions, however. All I suggested was a walk on the beach, and you talk about going to bed where you'll be safe. You'd think you were a young version of Sophia Loren or something. I was merely—you know—trying to be nice."

"So, I misspoke. You getting mad because I want to go to bed? C'mon, Parker. We're both smashed, you know that."

"This conversation's going nowhere," said Parker, turning away.

"You're right. I'm going nowhere . . . just safely to bed. Is that all right?"

"Go to bed. Who cares! I brought a manuscript from the slush pile. You can curl up with that and feel real safe!"

Meaghan disappeared into her room and closed the door. Firmly. Feeling rebuffed and a bit remorseful about his rather caustic remark to Meaghan, Parker walked to a nearby window and looked out over the weed-filled garden that surrounded Shady Gardens. His thoughts turned to Sarah. He'd harbored hopes, however remote, of seeing her at one of the large parties they'd attended. It was unlikely, since the functions seemed to consist mostly of publishing and entertainment people, and

Sarah was more of the old guard. Still, he could not be sure. She surfaced at unpredictable times.

Suddenly feeling himself drowsing, he retired to his room where he lay in bed on his back looking at the ceiling. Light from the moon came through an open window reflecting off a far wall. In one corner he noticed a small spider spinning a web. He watched as the insect diligently pursued its work, relentlessly moving about over the thin strands. For an instant he thought of taking a towel and wiping the web from the wall. After watching the spider's laborious efforts for several minutes, however, he was disinclined to destroy its work.

His thoughts returned to Sarah. Could she be in East Hampton? Maybe at the Maidstone Club. Was she with a date? Perhaps a boyfriend. . . . He listened to the distant rhythmic sound of the surf. How nice it would be to walk the beach with her. During their lunch in the elevator he'd sensed she was attracted to him; that she enjoyed being with him. But she still seemed strangely aloof; she was the one who would initiate any contacts.

Reflecting on his day at the shore, his thoughts turned to his mother. She'd always enjoyed the Hamptons; mostly South Hampton where she'd been a popular guest at large parties. It had not always been so. Her first marriage to his father, a car salesman, had been strained. Her part-time job as a model had helped, but the combined income barely satisfied family needs at their modest two-bedroom apartment in Tribeca, to say nothing of the wardrobe she required for so-called professional reasons. Family finances were always of concern, and the stress on his father probably contributed to a heart attack and early death.

Parker's mother had learned from experience. Two quick marriages had followed. First, to an older business tycoon that ended within a year, yielding significant rewards, and then to a rich young man more her age. The latter union had seemed on solid ground until his mother's death a short time later. Doctors and confidants had attributed her death to possible suicide resulting from depression, a condition seemingly brought on in part over concern for her fading beauty.

As he mentally flipped through the catalogue of earlier years he sensed the impending despair that accompanied such thoughts. He must think of something else. Tomorrow. Yes, a new day. A new time. The sweeping nature of time rendered problems almost meaningless. He turned on his side, closed his eyes, and listened to the relentless surf at the end of Potato Ridge.

CHAPTER 11

It was after Labor Day; summer was ebbing. An unusually cool night for early fall brought intimations of impending winter. There had been no sign of Sarah. She had vanished, a bewitching phantom perhaps never to reappear.

Candida had seemed preoccupied in recent days, less attentive to office matters. Parker had noticed a difference in their relationship as well, and it had prompted him to ask Meaghan if she had noticed the change in their boss. Meaghan had been oddly noncommittal, as if aware of the difference, but unwilling to share information. The variation in office mood had induced some paranoia in Parker. Had he done something wrong? Had they found out about his novel? Was Candida thinking of discharging him? Once provoked, his suspicions were limitless.

He stepped from his taxi on Fifth Avenue, and hesitated, looking across the street into Central Park. He stood for a while, considering going to the bench and relaxing. But after watching the cool breeze rustling the leaves on the other side of the road, he turned and walked to his building. At the entrance he exchanged greetings with the doorman, and he thought of asking about the young woman in the penthouse. Hesitating, and then impulsively, he said, "I have a question—"

"I beg your pardon, sir?" said the doorman quietly.

"I was wondering if you'd seen Miss Holloway who—" began Parker, raising his voice over passing traffic.

"I'm sorry, sir," said the man, leaning forward, his hand cupped to his ear.

Parker was uncertain. Was the man pretending not to hear? Or perhaps he was hard of hearing. Lord knows, hearing difficulties seemed to abound in the building. Halfway through the entrance, he deemed it unwise to persist with his question. "A bit chilly tonight," he offered, raising his voice and continuing into the building.

"Yes, yes indeed," said the doorman, closing the door softly.

And then, as he was nearing the elevator, a light melodious voice . . . in the hallway from beyond the dining room. He felt his spirits soar. Could it be she? No, it was his imagination again. He had to control his emotions better.

"Hi there, Parker. Need a lift?"

The words gripped him. It was the voice about which he'd dreamed. With quickening pulse, he moved into the darkened hallway. There, standing in the dim light of the old elevator, was Sarah. She was strikingly beautiful, yet something about her struck him as a bit unusual. Was it her clothes? Her hair?

"Well, Sarah . . . what a pleasant surprise." Regaining composure, he moved forward, stepping into the car. "Doing a little moonlighting I see. How's the elevator job?"

"Great. Not only that, you meet some terrific people," she said, closing the door. "What floor, sir?" Not waiting for an answer she pushed the button for the 23rd floor.

"I'll take that as a compliment," he said, encouraged by her friendly manner. "How did you know I was here in the building?"

"Saw you as you left your cab. Sometimes I see you from upstairs; when you get off the bus or come out of the park. Better be careful. Never know who's watching. So, how have you been?"

"Fine. I spent some time in the Hamptons since I last saw you. Didn't you mention that you go to the Hamptons?"

"Occasionally."

As they rose in the elevator he thought desperately of some way to make a more definite connection with her. She was quite close in the car, looking up at him, and he could feel her breath on his face. What he found exciting, even arousing, was that she did not seem at all concerned by their closeness.

"Seems I never see you," he continued, emboldened by their proximity. "I don't even know how to reach you. I thought of asking the ladies at the desk, but they're pretty careful about people's privacy. . . . Frankly, it would be nice to see you more often. . . ."

"I'm a working girl, remember?" she said facetiously, patting the elevator dial. "Actually, I'd like that, Parker," she added with a smile.

It was a response for which he had hoped, and as the car moved to his floor, he decided to go for it. "How about dinner some night . . . or a movie? . . . Unless you're tied up. . . ." he added diffidently. When she didn't immediately answer, and the car came to a halt on his floor, he added, "I hope I'm not being presumptuous, Sarah—"

"No, not at all," she replied quickly, coming against him as the door opened. "I enjoy seeing you, Parker. Very much. Probably more than you know. It's just . . . well, there are a few things. . . ." Once more she hesitated. "I'm going away tomorrow. I'm not sure when I'll be back. . . ."

And then to his astonishment, she patted him gently on the shoulder, and kissed him lightly on the cheek. "But I'll be back," she added, firmly, squeezing his hand. "I love being with you, Parker." It was almost as though she were concerned for him and trying to comfort him.

As the door slowly closed he glimpsed a partial reflection of himself standing alone in the elevator mirror. For Parker it was a most soulful and bewildering moment. He remained in front of the closed door, listening to the creaks and groans of the antique elevator fading into its past.

❖ ❖ ❖

CHAPTER 12

"**A** dickless tracy!"

"A what?" asked Parker.

"You know, a *woman*. The private detective is a *woman*."

Parker was at a bar near their office with Meaghan, who was offering sotto voce her point of view on their employer's romantic activities. It seems Candida had been secretly dating the CEO of one of Manhattan's larger publishing houses. Problems had surfaced with the relationship. The CEO was married and Candida suspected that they were being surveilled by a private investigator hired by a suspicious wife.

Parker sometimes met with Meaghan at the bar for an after-hours cocktail on his way home. Such infrequent meetings had kept him apprised of the comings and goings of their office to which he normally might not have been privy. He regarded such encounters with ambivalence, since he was concerned about how much of their discussions might be divulged to Candida. And although he liked Meaghan, he thought of her as a bit raffish, particularly her use of profanity, which at times was startling. The revelations about Candida's latest adventures, however, he found riveting.

Not only was Meaghan's information fascinating, it explained the change he sensed about interoffice relationships, and relieved the concerns he had about how they related to him. It was certainly understandable that Candida's tenuous position with her lover would manifest itself in her daily office activities. It surprised him that, given her wily and self-serving nature, she would allow herself to be drawn into such an illicit affair. How would it affect their agency? Their jobs? Still, having witnessed his boss's survival skills first hand, he'd bet on her ability to emerge unscathed. Indeed, she'd probably come out a winner in some way; probably pursuing litigation against the wayward lover for seduction or breach of promise. No, he sure wouldn't want to tangle with Candida inside or outside of court. It was worth bearing in mind as an aspiring author.

"Man," said Parker. "How in the world does she get involved in such things?"

"She does it for business," said Meaghan. "She doesn't give a damn about the guy. He's twice her age. She just likes to be seen with him at places like the Four Seasons and the Hamptons. Thinks it's good for her business image."

"I don't know about that," mused Parker. "It won't help her image much when she ends up in divorce court and the tabloids get hold of it. We'll probably all end up with subpoenas. You know how women are about these things—"

"Whataya mean, women?" interrupted Meaghan, bristling.

"Well, you know, wives can make it tough for men who, you know, just—"

"Are you kidding me? That old fart is an alley cat. Everyone knows it."

"Yes, but you know Candida," said Parker. "She's pretty active herself out there in the Hamptons. Some people wonder how she gets to all these exclusive parties. . . . And believe me, there's lots of guesses."

"You guys are all the same," said Meaghan, now coming to the defense of her boss. "So, sometimes she's a little aggressive. It's always the same with you guys. It's always all about sex."

"What? I never said anything about sex." Parker sensed the conversation going south. "All I said was—"

"Yeah, but I know where you were headed," she interrupted, draining the rest of her martini. "You guys all have the same thing in mind."

What Parker had most in mind at the moment was how to get out of the bar. Given her present mood, he knew from experience that a second martini with Meaghan could lead to trouble.

"Yeah, you're probably right," he said, glancing at his watch. "I better get going."

"Wherc you going?" she asked, annoyed.

"Have to meet a cousin of mine," he replied. He'd have to be careful. He might be using the cousin excuse too frequently.

"Yeah," said Meaghan wryly, abruptly grabbing her purse. "Remember, sit on that Candida stuff. Else we'll be meeting at the unemployment office."

"Of course," replied Parker. "Incidentally, how did you hear all that about Candida?"

"Telephone mostly. You know how she is on the phone. She starts off whispering, but when she gets worked up, she's like a jackhammer."

"Sounds as if she's got a lot to worry about," said Parker.

"Yeah, don't we all. If this crap hits the fan we're all in trouble. Could affect our business big time. That guy's a real dickhead."

Parker didn't reply, but sat quietly looking down at his martini. Meaghan's language was sometimes right out of the locker room. His mother would not have approved. And then impulsively, perhaps motivated by alcohol, he said, "You know, Meaghan, sometimes your language isn't very refined." It was an idle comment, but no sooner made than he regretted it.

"What!" from Meaghan, looking up sharply. "What's not refined about it?"

"Oh, I don't know. Just a passing thought. Well, you know . . . it's not . . . well, we're in the literary business . . . into language. Don't you think we should try to express ourselves with a little more—"

"Oh, you mean like those fancy broads on the Upper East Side." Meaghan reached for her purse. "Why don't you confine your drinks to those rich bitches up there rather than spending time with us bourgeoisie."

"Now really, Meaghan. I'm sorry. I didn't mean to. . . ."

"What makes you think your money and fancy background give you the right to criticize other people's language?" she snapped.

Parker was taken aback. It was clear his comment had unleashed some of Meaghan's pent-up feelings. "Meaghan, just a second. You've got it all wrong. I didn't grow up rich and all that. . . . Actually, my father was a car salesman. We had no real money or anything. After he died my mother was married a couple of times and came into some money—not all that much, really. I ended up with her apartment and a small trust—barely enough to keep the apartment going. Your idea that I come from some kind of wealth or something is. . . ." His voice trailed off. He'd talked too much. The martinis. . . . "Listen, Meaghan, I'm sorry. I didn't mean to offend you. Honestly."

There was little time for recovery, his words lost on the shapely form that bustled from the restaurant.

CHAPTER 13

It was a perfect night for a mugging. A cool dark evening, no moon, few visitors in a remote section of the park. But it was the last thing on Parker's mind as he sat on the bench reflecting on Sarah's absence from 822 Fifth Avenue. And so it was a jolting surprise when he glanced up at the dark, hooded figure who emerged from the blackness demanding his wallet.

"What?" he asked, gathering his wits. "What did you say?"

"Money," repeated the man. "This a stickup!"

"A what?" repeated Parker, staring into the darkness, his pulse quickening.

"A heist, man!" repeated the intruder. "Gimme yo money!"

"Oh, sure, sure," said Parker, reaching quickly into the inside pocket of his jacket.

"Easy, easy!" commanded the robber as he watched Parker

groping for his wallet. He shoved a serious-looking metallic object into Parker's stomach. "Only thing comin' outta there is yo money, unnerstan'?"

"No, no," said Parker, quickly. "Only the wallet. Say, uh . . . any chance of my keeping my wallet? Family pictures and all. . . . You can take the cash and—"

"Naw, no chance, chief," replied the robber.

"How about leaving me fifty bucks, then? So I can get by until morning?" persisted Parker. "I've gotta get something to eat and—"

"Hey, man, I ain't yo ATM. Don't yo unnerstan'? Yo bein' robbed!"

"Yeah, I know," replied Parker. "It's just I wanted to get a sandwich somewhere. There's nothing in my apartment to eat and—"

"Sorry, chief," said the robber. "I gotta eat too, y'know." He started to walk away, wallet in hand, then hesitated. Reaching into the wallet, he withdrew a fifty dollar bill, handing it over his shoulder without looking back. "Here, chief! Y'owe me fifty."

The following morning Parker recounted his mugging experience to Meaghan, who appeared to have recovered from her previous indignation in the restaurant. He commented on the generosity of the robber who had given back the fifty dollars. "See, no one's all that bad. It just goes to show—"

"What?" interrupted Meaghan who had listened unsympathetically. "Are you crazy? He robbed you of a couple of hundred bucks, and you're saying he wasn't that bad? He could've killed you. Stay outta that freakin' park at night."

>>> <<<

During ensuing days, Parker paid little attention to her warning, continuing his visits to the bench in Central Park always with the hope of seeing Sarah. A fortnight passed without incident, and he was sitting on the same park bench when a familiar voice came from the darkness.

"Hey, chief. Y'got my fifty bucks?"

Parker watched in disbelief as the hooded figure emerged from the darkness. "What? What are you talking about?"

"The fifty!" said the man. "'Member, I loan you fifty, couple weeks ago."

"You *loaned me*?" said Parker in disbelief. "You robbed me of two hundred dollars."

"Yeah, but that was a different transaction, chief. Gimme the fifty," he commanded, rummaging ominously in his pocket.

"I can't believe this," said Parker, withdrawing a money clip and handing over the fifty dollars. "Only in New York," he muttered.

"Whoa, gimme all of it," said the man, snatching the clip.

"What?" said Parker. "You said fifty."

"Interest. Thanks, chief," said the robber, disappearing into the foliage.

The next morning Parker reported the experience to Meaghan, who found the episode incomprehensible. "But why do you go back to the same spot? You shouldn't be in the park at night, everyone knows that."

"I always go there. It's a bench right off the exit on Fifth

Avenue where I live. I've never had any problems before." Parker shrugged his shoulders. "Anyway, he didn't seem like a bad guy. Besides, I found my wallet later on. . . . In the bushes near where he robbed me. He must have dropped it."

"What?" Meaghan interrupted, rolling her eyes toward the ceiling. "Candida's probably right. You're kind of kooky, you know that? I sometimes wonder if you don't just imagine all this crap. You sure this happened?"

"Of course it happened. Why would I make up such—"

"It's just that some of the things you say sound so weird. Why would a mugger give you back fifty bucks in the first place? It's all so strange."

"Meaghan, this is New York, remember? Anything can happen. Unbelievable things happen here every day. It's just another day at the office for that guy. He doesn't even realize he's doing anything wrong."

Meaghan turned away and picked up a paper on her desk, seemingly unconvinced. "Sure, whatever you say. Sometimes I wonder about you. These screwy stories. . . ."

Parker turned as if to go toward his office, then hesitated. "Anything new on our diva?" he asked, motioning with his head toward Candida's empty office.

Meaghan gave a short shake of her head, nodding toward Clara, a recently hired intern who sat at a distant desk. "Careful," she said softly. "Incidentally, you got a call from an Ada."

"Ada?" asked Parker, curiously. "Oh, Ada Collier. She submitted a manuscript several weeks ago."

"Didn't sound like an author," said Meaghan coyly. "She seemed to know you quite well."

"What are you implying, Meaghan?" said Parker, with appraising eyes.

"Girlfriend?" she asked without looking up.

"I have no girlfriend," he replied, caustically. "If I did, wouldn't everyone know it?"

"Maybe. Maybe not. You seem pretty quiet about your social life. Those high society broads up there on the East Side."

It was obvious Meaghan was on a fishing expedition. He knew from experience the best way to silence her queries was to put her on the defensive. "How about you? Do you have a boyfriend?"

"I've got lots of friends, some who are boys," she said, dismissively.

Parker saw a no-win situation looming. Meaghan was probably still simmering over his comment about her bad language. The one person he could not afford to reoffend at this particular time in his professional life was Meaghan. "How about we step out for some coffee a little later?" he asked.

"Let's see what happens around here," was the response.

More recovery time was needed with Meaghan, but he sensed it was okay. They'd have coffee.

CHAPTER 14

"Candida thinks you may be writing a book!" Meaghan's statement, coupled with her sly look, caught Parker by surprise. The two were having a mid-morning coffee break at a shop across the street from their office.

Parker looked up from his cup, startled. Then, feigning ignorance, he said, "Where in the world did she get that idea?"

"Well, you are, aren't you?" Meaghan's wily eyes bored in. "Candida said you went to the Iowa Writers' Workshop, and that everyone who goes there ends up writing books."

"That's absurd," countered Parker. "When would I have time to write a book? The way she heaps work on us. . . . Do you have any time to write books?"

"She wants to see your book," said Meaghan, ignoring his question.

"What? This is ridiculous." Parker felt the creeping panic. "Where in blazes do you people get your ideas? How could I be writing a novel when—"

"I didn't say it was a *novel*," interrupted Meaghan. "So, it's a *novel*! I could care less. All I'm saying is she wants to see it. If I were you I'd let her see it. Otherwise . . . you know, she might think you're hiding something. Look, I'm just trying to be helpful. You know Candida. One way or another, she's going to see your book."

Parker tried to suppress his emotions. He was no match for the street-savvy Meaghan and he knew it. He'd already blown his cover and Meaghan had pounced on it. Having averted his eyes and taken several gulps of coffee, he sat quietly considering his next move.

"Maybe you should destroy it." Now confident in her suspicions, Meaghan was in solution mode.

"What?" exclaimed Parker in amazement. "What are you talking about?"

"Your novel. Maybe you should get rid of it. If it's as bad as I'm beginning to think, maybe you should deep-six the bloody thing. Is Candida in the book?"

"Oh, boy. You two are something," said Parker, desperately. "I'm beginning to think I'm working with two paranoid—"

"Parker!" she interrupted. "You can't bullshit me. I've seen how secretive you are with your laptop and stuff. Now after listening to you deny it, I'm convinced you're writing a book. Am I in it? I bet I am. In fact, I want to see the thing, too. Am I in it?" she repeated, her voice rising.

Thoroughly undone by Meaghan's unrelenting questions, he wondered if he shouldn't just cop a plea. Own up to it and see if she'd help him with Candida. Maybe say he started a book but gave up on it. That's it, started a book but threw it away. With all the work at the agency, no time left to write a book. Meaghan wouldn't buy it of course, but maybe she'd help him with Candida. He couldn't take them both on. He needed an ally.

"Okay, Meaghan, you're a buddy, right? I'm going to tell you the truth—"

"I already know you're *not* going to tell me the truth," Meaghan interrupted, brushing her blonde hair back with a brief stroke. "Why don't you just tell me straight out? Forget all the nonsense."

"God!" he exclaimed, slapping the table with his hand. "I was about to tell you everything. You're impossible."

"Okay, okay," she said, pretending to understand. "Go ahead, tell me everything. But if you lie, I'm not going to sit here and just listen to a lot of crap."

Parker put his head back in exasperation. It was no use. Meaghan was 120 pounds of lie detection. Those penetrating eyes could look straight into his soul. "Okay, all right, you asked for it. But just remember, you tell anyone and I'm done." He paused a moment, the picture of someone poised at a chasm preparing to jump, and then, "You're right. I am sort of writing a book. It's all about time. The illusive nature of time. How things happen, but do they really happen? Is it all real or just an illusion? You know what I mean?"

"Is Candida in it?" Meaghan, never wasting words, went straight for the gut. "'Cause if she is, *your time* is *up*. Is she in it?"

"Well . . . maybe. Just a passing reference."

"Is there anything about her dating that guy, and the private dick I told you about?"

"Well. . . ." Parker's eyes floated about, trying to find anything to focus on other than Meaghan. "Maybe . . . but hardly anything at all. . . ."

"Holy shit," from Meaghan. "What about me? Anything about me?"

"Well. . . ."

"Don't try to bullshit me, Parker," the eyes now conveying green fire. "What's in that thing about me?"

"Hardly anything at all. You're barely . . ." (bad word, he had to watch himself) ". . . I mean you're *hardly* mentioned. You know . . . novels have to have a little romance and—"

"Jeez!" Meaghan's head dropped. "I wanna see that thing right now. Else Candida's gonna get an earful!"

"Okay. I understand," said Parker quickly. How in the world did the word *romance* come out? He was a terrible liar. "Don't worry about it," he said, picking up the check. "The book isn't going anywhere. I'll rip it up tonight. . . . Incidentally, this is all between you and me, right? Don't mention it to Candida, will you? Say, uh . . . how about a movie some night?"

There was no answer, the unwavering eyes having fixed him firmly in their sights. It was all over. He couldn't handle both Candida and Meaghan. It would be like crawling into the ring at the same time with Hulk Hogan and Stone Cold Austin.

CHAPTER 15

Having rumbled up twenty-three floors from where it languished undisturbed, the elevator was now quiet as a crypt. Indeed, the stillness was so pronounced that Parker found it disquieting. He had entered the car to work on his novel, and always with the thought that, however remote, it might lead to a meeting with Sarah. His immediate concern was how to protect the novel from the highly suspicious eyes of Meaghan and Candida. His only salvation, he thought, was a complete rewrite of those passages that involved the women. In fact, now confronted with Meaghan's blistering displeasure, he wondered how he could have written what he had in the first place. Although the main theme of his novel concerned the nature of time, the work had succumbed to digressions that had little to do with the story line—a common failing of first-time novelists. The result, casting Candida and Meaghan in tawdry roles, was unfortunate. Indeed, at one point he had even considered making them *lovers*, to juice up sexy portions in a struggling story line!

Reclining on the bench, head on the cushion from his apartment, manuscript on his lap, he had struggled to balance his thoughts between his novel and his ever-present feelings about Sarah. Several days had passed since their last contact. Had she gone to Europe? Come back? He had thought about inquiring in the building, but had restrained himself. It seemed implicit during their previous encounters that she would be the one to initiate any contact.

Unable to concentrate, he rose, preparing to leave the elevator, when he glimpsed a small, shiny object protruding from a corner beneath the bench. At first he thought it was a metal fixture, a small screw or fastening of the bench, but upon closer scrutiny he saw that it was a girl's ring. Perhaps Sarah had dropped it inadvertently, he thought, although he had never noticed rings on her fingers.

Overcoming his surprise, his first inclination was to replace it on the cushion, but after reflection concluded that if it were Sarah's it might be too important to leave unattended. To bring it to the attention at the front desk, however, would precipitate awkward questions about his off-limits presence in the elevator. There was another possibility; he could bring it up to her apartment, which he presumed was the penthouse. It was a perfectly legitimate reason for going there. If no one were at home he could slip it under the door or leave it in some receptacle. At least it offered a legitimate possibility of learning more about Sarah. But wouldn't it be imposing for him to go to her apartment unannounced? What if it were not her ring? She might consider it all a ruse on his part. . . . Finally, he pushed the top button and waited with considerable uncertainty as the car lumbered upward, coming to a jolting halt at the top floor.

A dim light shone in the lobby outside a door which he assumed led to the penthouse. It was very still, and as he stepped from the elevator he was gripped by a strange sensation, a feeling similar to what he had experienced in the basement weeks before—that there was something nearby, watching. . . .

Observing a bell next to the door, he walked over and pushed it gently. There was no answer. Again he pushed the bell and was considering whether to leave when slowly, almost cautiously, the door opened a few inches.

"Yes? May I help you?" came a woman's voice.

Parker could partially see the silhouette of a mature woman in what appeared to be a maid's white domestic uniform. "Yes, ma'am. May I speak with Sarah?

"I beg your pardon?" said the woman.

"Sarah. Is this Sarah Holloway's apartment?" repeated Parker awkwardly, finding it difficult to communicate with the woman through the partially opened door.

"No. I'm sorry, sir. You have the wrong place. This is the Thatcher apartment."

"Thatcher?" said Parker, confused. "I was told this was—"

"I'm sorry," the woman interrupted with a touch of irritation. "Perhaps you should check with the front desk." She moved as though to close the door.

"But . . . may I speak with Miss Thatcher?" blurted Parker, now grasping for understanding.

"I'm sorry, sir. Miss Thatcher is in repose." She then closed the door, slowly but resolutely.

Parker stood motionless for a moment, looking at the closed door. Recovering, he looked around the lobby. Was he on the right floor? Was there another apartment? There didn't seem to be any other doors. Perhaps there was an entrance to another apartment from the regular elevator. That was probably the case. At any rate, his lingering in the foyer might worry the maid. Residents were ordinarily informed of guests by the front desk, and it was understandable that his appearing unannounced in a remote section of the building would be of concern to the maid.

Once back in the elevator, he closed the door and pushed the button for his floor. As he rattled his way down, he gazed at the ring fondly. Just the thought of it having been on her hand was stirring. The elevator thumped to a stop at his floor. Rather than leave the car, he dropped down on the bench, reclining against the wall, reflecting on Sarah. Maybe the day would come when he could give her a ring. Perhaps an engagement ring. She *had* actually kissed him and told him she loved being with him. He sensed she liked him. If there were only some way he could spend more time with her. It could lead to all manner of things. An engagement . . . marriage. . . . Yes, a wedding.

He rested his head back, consumed by the dream. It would be a church wedding. Soft organ music floating from the choir. The arrival of the bridesmaids. Finally, radiant in her gown, would be Sarah. It was enchanting whimsy. Had the angel intaglios on the church walls come singing to life, it could not have been more heavenly. . . .

❖ ❖ ❖

CHAPTER 16

"Let's see it!"

"What?" said Parker. "See what?" But he knew.

"You know damn well what!" Meaghan had had time to reflect on his novel, and she was in shoot-out mode. It was a battle Parker could never win.

"Look, Meaghan," he whimpered. "We're friends, aren't we? Keep your voice down," his eyes glancing toward Clara at the far side of the room. "Where's Candida?"

No response from Meaghan, who wore the expression of someone who'd just learned her fiancé was transgender.

"I can't believe you're so upset over a silly novel," continued Parker.

"I'm a sex object in your book," from Meaghan.

"That's absurd," continued Parker. "Besides, the book is done with. Finished. All over!"

There was some truth to his statement. The book could be truly "all over" since he'd inadvertently left his hard copy on a Madison Avenue bus during the weekend. His name and return address were clearly marked on the manuscript box, but enormously troubling was the fact that it was the office address on West 51st Street. What made it truly cataclysmic, and had the potential of career-ending ramifications, was that most incoming mail at the office was handled by none other than Meaghan. Much of the mail was composed of unsolicited manuscripts that Meaghan afforded cursory attention. However, one bearing the return address of Parker Livingstone would be tantamount to striking gold. Chances that the designation PERSONAL marked on the manuscript box would deter Meaghan were remote. If Parker needed an ally at this stage of the crisis, it was clear who it was.

"Meaghan, how about a drink tonight?"

"We'll see," was the cool response.

Things warmed up during the day at the office. Parker brought Meaghan some coffee; commented on an attractive scarf she was wearing; complimented her on some editing she'd done on a young adult book. Candida wasn't at the office. Parker's question whether she'd be coming in was answered with another "we'll see." It was apparent Meaghan sensed she had the upper hand. It was almost five p.m. before she opened up. "We having our drink?"

"You betcha," said Parker, relieved. Once in the bar, Meaghan would be all talk. One martini, two if needed, and he'd know more about Candida's problems than Candida.

Meaghan had mellowed a bit by the time they sat down at their usual table in the corner of the restaurant. "I think I'll just have a club soda tonight," she said as the waiter approached.

"Whoa," thought Parker. Not according to plan. "How about a margarita?" He said jovially. "Loosen you up a bit. You seem a little tense."

"Make it a martini," she said to the waiter. "Very dry, with an olive."

"Make it two," from Parker, relieved. Leaning back in his chair, he spoke a bit about his weekend: a walk in the park, dinner at Eileen's with a buddy from college, a matinee at a nearby theater . . . some of which was true. With the arrival of the martinis he began laying the groundwork for the serious stuff.

"Boy, that was really some heavy editing you did on that young adult manuscript. I liked the way you handled those digressions. . . ." And so it went.

After a few gulps of her martini, Meaghan had had enough of his solicitude. "You sound like a guy who's trying to get laid," she said flatly. "What's on your mind, Parker?"

Parker drew back, rolling his eyes. "Really, Meaghan, you're something else. That's not very ladylike, you know."

"Well, I know you've got something on your mind," she said, green eyes hardening. "Why don't you just say it without all the crap?"

Parker knew it was hopeless. He sat quietly for a moment, then took a sip of his martini. "What's new with Candida?"

"Lots."

"Well, what's *lots*?" he asked, finishing off his martini and motioning to the waiter for refills.

"You're trying to get me stoned, right?" said Meaghan. "So I'll tell you everything about Candida . . . more stuff for your book, right?"

"C'mon, Meaghan. What's with you? We're supposed to be buddies. I told you, the book's over with. It's done. Gone forever. Forget it, will you?"

Meaghan took a swallow of her martini. "Her looney boyfriend's been served with papers. Candida's named in the divorce suit. Just a question of time before it hits *Page Six*," she said, referring to a popular gossip column in a New York paper.

"You're kidding," exclaimed Parker. "Wow. How's Candida taking it?"

"She's a nervous wreck. Wants us all to go to the Hamptons this weekend for a rest. And forget that tickle in your throat crap."

"There's no way I can go to the Hamptons this weekend," said Parker, his brow knitted. "I've already made plans."

"Forget them, if you want to continue with the Jones Agency. Candida's been shacking up with her boyfriend at Shady Gardens. She writes off much of the stuff out there as a business expense, and she has to show we all go out there regularly for meetings."

"Are you kidding me?" Parker exclaimed. "I can see how we're going to get dragged into that divorce battle. You can't tell where this will end up. You can't lie in court about this stuff. You could go to jail!"

"Yeah, I can see why you're worried. You're not bad lookin'. I can see where doing time could be tough on you," she said with a smirk.

"This is no laughing matter, Meaghan." Parker shifted in his chair and took another swig of his martini. "Once you're named in a divorce suit, there's no telling where it will end up. Divorce lawyers will put into play anything they can to embarrass defendants. . . . Pressure them to settle."

"Well, that's Candida's problem," said Meaghan.

"It could be a problem for all of us if she asks us to lie to save her. Don't you see, Meaghan? These things take on a life of their own. I don't see how she can write off that potato field out there as a business expense. I know something about divorce from my mother."

"Your mother?" Meaghan's eyes lit up. "What happened? Tell me about it."

Parker realized his mistake immediately. His mother would be of intense interest to Meaghan. "I already told you about my mother, remember," he said, raising the martini glass to his lips. "Don't you understand, Meaghan? Some things are personal."

"Well, you brought it up. Why are you so secret about everything? You want me to tell you all I know about Candida, but when it comes to your own stuff you're a freakin' mute. Screw you, buddy!"

Meaghan's feathers had been ruffled and Parker knew he was in hostile territory. He could be sitting alone shortly unless he reclaimed her interest. "I'm sorry," he said, following another sip of his martini. "My mom and I were very close. It was pretty tough when my dad died. He didn't have much insurance. She then married a rich guy—it didn't last too long—big battle with his family over money. She remarried. Nice guy. She died a short time later. That's it. My mom and I were close. It's been pretty tough," he said, draining the last of his drink. "That's what started my depression."

"I'm sorry," said Meaghan, her own maternal instincts seeming to surface. "Is that why you're in therapy?"

"What! What therapy?" Parker, surprised, realized he'd talked too much and had had too much to drink. "What are you talking about?"

"Candida told me all about your therapy."

"Jesus! You people are really something," exclaimed Parker. "Isn't anything sacred in that office?"

"Well, not really," said Meaghan. "Remember, you're in the publishing business, and that's all about disclosure, right? And that brings me back to that novel of yours. If you think I did some heavy editing on that children's book, wait till you see what I do with that novel of yours."

Parker saw the need for a change in their conversation. "Whatever brought you into publishing?" he asked. "Did you study writing in college? Where'd you go to college?"

"Hunter."

"How about high school?" said Parker, anxious to keep the conversation off his therapy.

"Bleeker Hall."

"Bleeker Hall?" said Parker. "Is that in Manhattan?"

"Yeah," answered Meaghan.

"I don't think I've heard of it. What type of courses do they—"

"Survival," said Meaghan, interrupting.

"Survival?"

"Yeah. It's an orphanage."

"Oh," said Parker, momentarily surprised. Unsure how to respond he was almost ready to revive discussion about his novel.

"It's okay," said Meaghan. "You learn all about life real fast at Bleeker Hall. Sometimes cold, dangerous, uncertain. . . . I'm proud of it. Like climbing Mount Everest."

Parker was quiet, caught by a burst of feeling. He felt he was looking at someone he had never really known until that moment.

CHAPTER 17

Hi Sarah,

I hope this note finds you well and back from your trip. I found a ring in the old elevator that possibly belongs to you. I would like to return it at your convenience. I continue to look for you in the dining room, and even the old elevator, to no avail. I hope I'm not being too presumptuous, but it would be nice to see you again.

I trust I'm not intruding, but I've enjoyed our meetings. They've certainly been unusual, don't you agree? After all, how many people meet and lunch in an elevator?

Hope to see you sometime soon. Until then, my best wishes.

Sincerely,
Parker Livingstone

Parker had agonized over the note for two days, wondering if he should send it to the penthouse. Following his meeting with the maid, he'd determined by riding the regular elevator that there was, indeed, only one penthouse. At first surprised, he'd concluded that Sarah was probably just a visitor there, and this would have explained her hesitancy when volunteering information. Contributing to his dilemma was the fact that one of the ladies at the front desk had mentioned to him that she'd been contacted by the maid in the Thatcher apartment relative to an unannounced visitor, presumably Parker. The brief, direct exchange confirmed that unannounced visits were unwelcome in the building. The discussion with the front desk had done little for his confidence, and, given these developments, he'd elected to discard the letter.

The experience, while disheartening, had not diminished his feelings for Sarah. There had been other girls, but there had never been anyone who'd captured him so completely. His mother had always been the center of his emotions, his very soul, but this was different. From that first moment in the park, as brief as it was, he'd been enchanted, his feelings intensifying with successive contacts. A day never passed that she was not the center of his thoughts. Whatever love was, it had enveloped him.

As the days passed his uncertainties increased. Had he been too aggressive? Asking for a date? Intruding at the penthouse? The fallout at the front desk. . . . A person such as she would be pursued relentlessly by admirers. Was there someone else? She hadn't mentioned anyone when he asked for the date in the park. Still, there must be someone. A girl with her charm. . . . He might well be wasting his time. Yet, she seemed attracted to him. The kiss on the cheek . . . but she'd been restrained. He sensed something else as well. A feeling as though she wanted to comfort him.

But there were other matters that demanded his attention. Problems at the office. He'd been able to avoid the trip to East Hampton. Candida had wanted to leave on Thursday for a long weekend, but a legitimate meeting with one of his authors had served as an excuse. With the distraction of impending legal problems involving her erstwhile consort, Candida was less demanding of her employees.

Of more immediate concern to Parker was the whereabouts of his novel. He lived in dire fear of the call from Meaghan announcing that his book had been found, and that she'd arranged personally to pick it up. Should that happen, it would be only a quick read to determine that she and Candida had been cast as the "sex objects" she'd envisioned. For him it would mean total banishment without redemption. His only hope was that she would come to him before going to Candida; something on which he could hardly rely. Maybe it would be best to come clean. Just tell her his characters had taken on lives of their own; that there was nothing at all personal in it. In fact, he could say he was rather surprised she saw any similarity between herself and the character in the novel. . . . No, that wouldn't work at all. The character was all Meaghan. Best he just hope the bloody thing had been discarded with the bus trash. He thought most of the manuscript had been preserved on his laptop.

It was late morning when his ragged emotions began to show. He was standing by a desk near his office when a telephone rang. He moved quickly to a nearby phone and lifted the receiver. "Candida Jones Agency. . . . No, I'm sorry she isn't here at the moment. May I take a message? . . . Yes, ma'am. . . . You're welcome. . . . Bye."

Meaghan, observing the transaction, was curious. "What was that about?"

"For Candida. No message," he replied.

"Why you answering the phone?" she asked. "Clara's here. You seem nervous."

Parker didn't reply. He had to be careful. Meaghan's instincts would be the envy of a psychic.

❖ ❖ ❖

CHAPTER 18

P arker sat on the bench, lost in the darkness that settled over the park. By day it was a cheerful area where
strolling urbanites sought relief in the 843 pastoral
acres at the center of Manhattan's throbbing metropolis. But
by nightfall, the dual character of the place became evident,
and it could change into a gloomy spot where strange images
huddled in the shadows, forewarning of predators lurking
beyond a bend in the path. The scene was especially forebod-
ing at the moment. Parker was sensitive to such matters, having
been robbed recently. Yet thoughts of Sarah had been with him
constantly, overcoming any desire to be elsewhere. She knew he
often spent time there, and it seemed a likely place for them to
meet. Suddenly, his thoughts were interrupted by the appearance of a figure shuffling toward him from down the path.

"Evening, son," came a voice.

As the person neared he was surprised to see the homeless man with whom he had conversed several weeks before. The man was unsteady and seemed to have been drinking. Expecting to be asked for money, Parker reached for his billfold.

"No, not necessary," said the man. "I'm okay. Mind if I join you for a second?" Not waiting for a reply, he placed a paper binder he was carrying on the end of the bench and settled down. "Walked all the way over from the West Side. Long walk for an old man."

"Of course. I was just leaving, anyway," Parker said, feeling a need to disengage.

"Don't let me chase you away," said the man. "Aren't you the chap that helped me out here awhile back? That was very nice of you. You come here quite often, do you?"

"Sometimes," Parker replied. Not wanting to become involved, but curious about the man's patrician manner, he was inclined to be more responsive than the occasion warranted. "I live close by so I rest here on occasion."

"Indeed," said the man, curiously. "Whereabouts?"

"Over there," said Parker with a slight motion of his head. And then, feeling a need to be more courteous, he added, "On Fifth Avenue."

"I used to have a lady friend, a girlfriend, on Fifth Avenue," said the man. "Years ago. In that building behind us. We used to sit on this bench."

Startled by the man's comment, Parker was unsure how to

respond. Did he mean Parker's building? Was the man telling the truth? Or did he simply want someone to whom he could talk? But his manner and delivery suggested a sincerity that would be difficult to feign. He vaguely recalled the man mentioning during a previous meeting that he had lost a girlfriend years ago. Although curious, he had to be careful. "Yes, this would've been a nice spot to meet," Parker said. "And you come here to this place . . . because of her, or . . . ?"

"Yes, she meant everything to me." He paused, reflectively, his head dropping slightly. Regaining his composure, he said, "She disappeared one day." Again his head dropped. "I come here to be near her. She said someday she'd be back."

His curiosity aroused, Parker focused on the man. "You mentioned a building, sir? You mean the one right behind us?"

"Well, I better go, son," said the man, ignoring his question. He rose unsteadily, then, turning, reached for the worn binder on the bench. "Can't forget my book."

"Book?" said Parker, inquisitively.

"Yes," said the man shuffling away. "Perhaps another time. . . ."

Parker sat motionless, confused, the homeless man's mutterings proving elusive in the darkness. He settled back on the bench, listening to a light breeze above in the trees. It seemed to him to be moaning intermittently, perhaps lamenting the passage of another day. Time was like the wind, he thought, invisible but resolute, changing the nature of things.

❖ ❖ ❖

CHAPTER 19

"There's someone on the phone who says she found a box with your name on it. Wants to know if there's a reward. She sounds a little . . . well, unusual."

Clara's announcement was attracting attention in the Candida Jones office. Parker's prompt "I'll take it!" followed by a studied nonchalance as he made his way to a nearby phone, had kindled Meaghan O'Reilly's instincts. Her desk was within earshot. Parker knew she had an appointment, and was hoping she'd leave.

The call was from a girl who had found a box with his name and telephone number. The cryptic voice asked if there were a reward for the box's return. Parker's effusive thanks and assurances of a reward were met with an abrupt "how much?" His suggestion that they discuss the reward when they met was rebuffed with a stiff "no number, no meetin'." Startled, Parker glanced over to where Meaghan was sitting nearby. The blonde head and blank expression locked on a computer did not fool him. He sensed precisely where Meaghan's attentions were at the moment. He had to get off the phone quickly. With an abundance of assurances, he finally convinced the girl to meet him at the information booth at Grand Central Terminal at eleven that morning.

"What was that about?" asked Meaghan as he hung up.

"Oh, nothing. Someone apparently found a misplaced package," he said, quickly putting on his jacket and preparing to leave.

"Want me to get it?" from Meaghan. "I have to go out, anyway."

"No, no," he replied, moving toward the door.

"But I'm going right by Grand Central," she persisted. "I can pick it up on my way to—"

Her words were lost as he slipped out. "Phew!" he thought as he reached the street. Meaghan had the ears of a jackal. But what was the difference? He'd already told her about his book.

He proceeded east on 51st Street with what he felt would be ample time to reach Grand Central. His optimism was dealt a blow when he reached Fifth Avenue and saw unusually heavy traffic. Because of the configuration of one-way streets, he realized that alternative routes could be exceedingly time consuming. With a nervous glance at his watch he elected to continue down Fifth Avenue, glancing continuously back over his shoulder for a taxi. He had walked almost two blocks when he spotted a cab being vacated several yards ahead. Claims to the taxi had apparently already been made by a middle-aged woman who was closer to the car than Parker. Under normal circumstances he would have deferred to the older woman, but with the recovery of his manuscript uppermost in mind, there were no options. What if the girl with the manuscript left before he arrived? She seemed quite young. Would she call again? If she did, would she reach Meaghan? Or Candida! No, it was no time for chivalry. Indeed, he'd climb in the cab *with* the woman if necessary.

Sprinting forward, he reached the taxi just as the woman was about to open the door. "Thank you. Thank you, madam. Sorry, this is an emergency," he said, briskly.

Startled, the woman stepped aside. "What?" she exclaimed. "This is my cab!"

"Sorry," repeated Parker. "Ordinarily I'd never do this. I hope you understand," he murmured.

There was no understanding, but rather a venomous "you bastard" from the older woman. Although he expected something less than a gracious exchange, he was surprised by her middle-finger salute as he sped away.

It was approaching eleven when he entered Grand Central. To his relief, he saw a teenaged girl holding what appeared to be his manuscript, standing among other people near the information counter. She had loosely hanging black hair, dark eyes, and, despite her young features, the brooding look of one who had already experienced life's darker side. He walked quickly to the girl and with a bright smile introduced himself.

"Louisa?" he asked, struggling to remember the name the girl had given him on the phone. "I'm Parker Livingstone," he said, holding out his hand.

"Lucretia," she corrected, avoiding his eyes and ignoring his hand.

"Well, it certainly is nice of you to return this," he said, reaching for the book. "I was afraid—"

"Reward!" commanded the girl, stepping back, holding the manuscript to her chest.

"Oh, of course," said Parker, taken aback by her abrupt manner. He reached into his jacket for his wallet. "Would twenty dollars be okay?" he asked, feeling generous under the circumstances.

"Fifty!" said the girl, without a beat.

"What?" said Parker, surprised. With a lift of his brow, he reached into his billfold and offered the girl the money.

She hesitated for an instant and then, "Hundred!"

Parker, stunned, stood holding the money out to her. "I beg your pardon," he said, lowering his voice. "That's a bundle of paper you have there. Not the family jewels. What do you think this is?"

"Okay, so you don't want it," said the girl, starting to move away.

"Wait, wait a second," Parker said, mind racing. He noted a nearby transit officer taking an interest in their transaction. The girl's next number could well be north of a hundred. "Here, here's the money," he said, quickly pulling the bills from his pocket and offering them to her.

The girl hesitated for a moment, seemingly evaluating his eagerness, then abruptly, took the money. "I'm probly gettin' screwed." Thrusting the manuscript at him, she turned, and walked away.

He exchanged a look with the police officer who continued to stare at Parker as he left the terminal.

Back at the office, an expectant Meaghan had no time for amenities. "So, did you get it?"

"Get what?" Parker barely stopped as he headed with the manuscript toward the safety of his office.

"You know damn well what!" shot Meaghan. "The goddam novel!"

Parker knew Meaghan had him in her sights and there was no way of avoiding a major confrontation. Clara would have told her in detail about the earlier call concerning the recovery of the manuscript. There was little choice. He had to have Meaghan's support.

"Yes, I have it," he acknowledged. "And I'm taking it straight to the shredder."

"Let's see it," commanded Meaghan.

"What?" said Parker, now thoroughly alarmed.

"Give me the goddamn manuscript! I want to see that freaking thing right now," exclaimed Meaghan, rising from her desk and moving toward him.

"Easy. Take it easy," he soothed, glancing toward Clara in the far corner.

Clara, having already experienced a few internecine office

battles, deemed it time for a visit to the ladies' room. As the door closed softly behind her, Parker headed for the office shredder with Meaghan closely behind.

"There," said Parker with finality, feeding leaves of the manuscript into the machine. "That's the end of the bloody thing. Satisfied?"

"Hold it! Wait a second," said Meaghan, peering over his shoulder. "There's nothing there!"

"What?" from Parker. "That's my novel."

"Just a minute," exclaimed Meaghan, grabbing a sheaf of pages and examining them closely. "Look," she exclaimed, holding them in front of Parker. "Blank pages. Can't you see? There's nothing there, there!"

CHAPTER 20

It was a quiet evening in Central Park. Visitors had departed earlier, and the usual vendors and street merchants had left for more lucrative venues. The animals in the zoo had been fed and bedded down for the night and, while predators not yet confined to cages could be making their customary rounds, there seemed little crime at the moment in the vicinity of Lenox Hill. Even the buzz of traffic on nearby avenues seemed distant and muted by the heavy foliage that hung low over the bench on which Parker rested. For an autumn evening it was unseasonably warm but, having removed his jacket, he was reasonably comfortable.

It had been an alarming day at the office. He had written down his novel, he was sure! Or was he? His offhand comment to Meaghan that the blank pages in his manuscript were because the novel was still largely in his head had left her highly suspicious and withdrawn. The fact that two of the agency's manuscripts had received offers from publishing houses that day had served to distract Meaghan, but Parker realized his strange behavior was an issue which had been tabled only momentarily. As for Candida, her other affairs continued to occupy her, and her visits from legal types had aroused the interest of her colleagues.

Parker's concerns were soon replaced by thoughts of his meetings with Sarah that always hovered on the fringe of consciousness, waiting to be revived. He wondered about her . . . where she was . . . what she was doing. . . . Was she in Europe? With someone else? In the arms of a lover? The last, a crushing thought, caused him to shift uncomfortably on the bench.

As he sat speculating about Sarah, he sensed the first stages of a creeping panic attack: a wave of fear, spinning sensation, nausea. Although infrequent, such seizures had been a part of his life since childhood, but were usually of short duration. Leaning forward, head in his hands, he struggled to restrain his emotions as confusing thoughts of his manuscript resurfaced.

Regaining control, his thoughts drifted back to Sarah; particularly the last encounter when she had kissed him on the cheek in the elevator. It had been entirely unexpected, leaving him with the impression that he could be underestimating her feelings for him.

Suddenly, his ruminations were interrupted by a voice from beyond the exit leading to the street. Was it Sarah? He listened intently. Yes, it was her voice—clear, distinct. He straightened and turned in the direction of the exit, his heart beating expectantly.

There, standing in the glow of a street lamp, her stunning beauty radiant even in the dim light, was Sarah.

"Hello, Parker. I thought I saw you coming in here," she said, her casual stride bringing her closer. "What have you been up to? I haven't seen you in a while."

"Sarah," he exclaimed exuberantly, standing quickly. "What a wonderful surprise!"

"It's great to see you," she said, taking his arm, and kissing him lightly on the cheek. "I've been thinking of you," she added with a friendly smile. "Lots!"

Parker, overcome by the unexpected kiss and encouraged by her affectionate manner, struggled to respond. "Here, come sit down," he said, guiding her toward the bench. "I've missed you. I thought maybe you'd gone to Europe."

"It's a long story." She took his hand, squeezing it slightly. "I don't think I realized how much I was going to miss you. I mean. . . ." Her eyes drifted off as if searching for words. "Well, it's so good to see you. I've thought about you quite often. Are things going well?"

"Yes, very well. Things seem to be picking up in the publishing world."

"That's nice to hear," she said. "How about your own book?"

"Well . . . that's a different story," he said, hesitating. "But let's talk about you. Where have you been? Frankly, I've thought about you . . . a great deal, actually. It would be nice to see you more often. . . . How about tonight? Would you like to go up to Eileen's for dinner?"

"I'm sorry, Parker. I'd love to. But I have someone waiting for me right now. I really would like to see you more often. Perhaps we could. . . ." she hesitated, her face very close to his. "But there are things I should mention. That is, my relationship with you. . . ." She paused as if considering her words. "Well . . . to be honest, I find you very attractive, Parker. In fact, I'd like very much to be with you, but. . . ." She squeezed his hand and leaned against him slightly as her voice trailed off.

At that moment he sensed from her a strong feeling of warmth and intimacy that exceeded his expectations. But her hesitancy about their relationship was puzzling. Was there someone else? Was she committed? Emboldened by her warm demeanor, he moved closer and spoke softly. "Sarah, you probably think I'm a strange duck—some kind of weird gypsy, hanging out in that old elevator and all. But I'm really just an average, normal guy—at least most of the time. You must know how I feel about you." As he looked into her eyes, she lifted her face toward him slightly in what seemed an enticing manner. Suddenly, spontaneously, he took both her hands and kissed her gently on the lips. When she responded ardently, and then pressed her cheek against his, Parker realized his life would never be the same.

"I love you, Sarah," he said, holding her hands tightly against him. "I think I've loved you since that first day I saw you here in the park. I've thought about you constantly. But it's all been so strange. . . ."

"I understand, Parker. I love you as well. It was the same for me that moment in the park when I first saw you. There was something about you that instantly caught my attention. Your eyes somehow conveyed a sense of sadness—that you were alone, having lost something precious. And then our meetings here in the park . . . the elevator . . . our lunch . . . I found myself falling in love with you. But I felt it was so terribly unfair to you. You see, Parker, there are things you must understand. I'm away a great deal. We come from different worlds. With me you'd be forgoing much of your own life. Like the theme of your book, love is deceiving, an illusion actually. It's like that song that came out not too long ago: 'Falling in Love with Love.'"

"Song?" said Parker, surprised and overcome by her revelation of love for him, but confused by her reticence. "I'm not familiar with it."

"You know, by Rodgers and Hart. It's from the show on Broadway, *The Boys from Syracuse*. Perhaps you'd like to see it. I can get you a ticket. The song has wonderful lyrics . . . goes like this." Softly, in an exquisite voice, she gently began to sing.

Falling in love with love is falling for make believe.
Falling in love with love is playing the fool.
Caring too much is such a juvenile fancy.
Learning to trust is just for children in school.

"And so on. . . ." she said, patting his arm affectionately.

Parker, captivated by her singing, recovered and said, "You have a remarkable voice. But the lyrics of the song . . . they sound a bit, I don't know . . . maybe a little sad."

"You're right," she said. "Very sad. But very true, I'm afraid. I really must go, Parker." She was standing now, moving toward the exit. Turning, she waved slightly. "Don't worry, Parker. I love you. I'll be back."

Rising from the bench, Parker acknowledged her wave. Elated by her expression of love, he waited momentarily until she had left the park. Then slowly he followed her toward the exit where he paused and watched as she crossed Fifth Avenue toward what appeared to be a vintage Rolls Royce limousine parked at the entrance to their building. Here a liveried chauffeur opened a rear door where she joined a masculine figure in the back seat. The limousine cautiously pulled away with a soft, rich purring sound. As he watched the car fading into the traffic, he was gripped by an intense sense of loneliness and wonder, the euphoria he'd experienced only moments before, upon hearing she loved him, tempered by the sight of the person in the limousine. Who was the man? A date, perhaps? A boyfriend? Where were they going? The limousine conveyed the aura of wealth. Given his own modest circumstances, how could he hope to exist in such a world of opulence?

He stood under the street lamp for a moment, gazing out at the steady stream of traffic along Fifth Avenue. Then, his thoughts in turmoil, he slowly returned to the bench and the deep solitude of Central Park.

❖ ❖ ❖

CHAPTER 21

Anna Baker was an accomplished therapist, having replaced her mentor several years before at their offices on Lexington Avenue. Following his mother's disappearance, Parker had become a patient of Anna's predecessor, and after some interruption had continued his sessions with Anna. Although Parker's diagnosis by the previous psychologist had been depression caused by his mother's disappearance at sea, Anna had diagnosed his chronic depression as having been exacerbated by a serious condition that had afflicted his mother—a Narcissistic Personality Disorder or NPD, an ailment which manifested in extreme egotism. Unfortunately for Parker, a consequence of his mother's NPD was a parent fixation often found in children of the afflicted which can result in other maladies. In Parker's case, according to Anna, it had resulted in a parent fixation causing severe depression that could lead to other disorders.

Although unable to understand completely the psychological ramifications, and somewhat skeptical of her diagnosis, Parker thought his sessions with Anna were beneficial. The counseling had continued intermittently for the previous few years and he now found himself in discussion with the therapist in her office.

"So, you're finally writing your novel," she said with an assuring smile. "Is it the same one you started at the Iowa writing school?"

"No, this is altogether different. There are a few leitmotifs to keep the story moving, but the major theme deals with time. The protagonist is a theoretical physicist. The story line deals with time as cyclical rather than linear, so that the protagonist ends up in an eternal cycle of renewal. It's like the proverbial snake devouring itself—a cyclical process and symbol of eternity. My protagonist eventually discovers that there's no ending for his novel. It sounds confusing, I know, but it's about the illusory nature of life. It's titled *Where Goes the Wind.*"

"Yes, but I thought we agreed that you'd concentrate less on time and—"

"Well, I find it therapeutic, to think about it. The more I think about time, the more convinced I become about the unreality of life." He shifted uncomfortably as he felt Anna's robotic eyes focusing on him. He had come to the point in their meetings where he could sense Anna's thoughts almost as well as she could read his. He realized from previous sessions that she found his preoccupation with time to be troubling. "I know you tire of me repeating these things, but you're the only one I dare confide—"

"No, no, Parker," she interrupted. "Please continue. It's important you tell me. The only way I can be helpful is if you—"

"It's difficult to explain," continued Parker, interrupting. "Abstract thoughts about time defy logical explanations. . . . Philosophers have been confounded by it through the ages. Marcel Proust, for example, who spent a lifetime exploring the subject. In *Swann's Way* he describes the four dimensions of space, the fourth being duration or time. But neither he nor anyone has been able to convey any real sense of clarity about the actual nature of time. It's one of life's most mystifying and elusive subjects. Some say it drove Nietzsche mad. The more I think or write about it, the more convinced I become about the unreality of life as we perceive it."

Parker paused, glancing at the ceiling. Was Anna finding his remarks incoherent, senseless perhaps? Whenever he'd expressed some of his views on the subject, she'd been reserved and noncommittal. But he had been careful, never expressing himself fully, concerned she would question his mental stability. Encouraged at the moment by her professed interest, however, he continued.

"There's no such thing as present time, Anna. It's a fallacy that governs our existence. There's only the past and future. Present time doesn't exist. And if there's no present, then there's no life or existence as we know it. The past is like dreams. Just memories. The same with the future, simply expectations. It's unreal. Perhaps it's a crude way of saying it, but life is almost a sham. Delusive, beguiling in a way, offering hope and promise of something that can never be. Einstein summed it up rather succinctly: 'Life is illusory.'"

He paused, looking directly at the therapist, attempting to evaluate her reactions. Was she listening? Or was she diagnosing some personality disorder on his part? Lord knows, it seemed as if clinical psychologists had a behavioral disorder for anything a patient might express outside the mainstream.

"That's an interesting concept, Parker." Anna shifted in her chair slightly, her eyes fixed on him in a nonconfrontational manner. "But when you say there's no present time . . . isn't this present time now as we sit here discussing the subject? I mean—"

"Not really," he interrupted. "What we think of as present time is so utterly ephemeral that it's nonexistent. No reality, as I said. If we could stop time, then we'd have a present time. But as long as time passes, all we have is the past and future. No present exists. The only thing that stops time in life is death. Existentialists such as Camus, Sartre, and many others have struggled with time issues, and someday a brilliant philosopher, or perhaps a theoretical physicist, will surface and express time in ways that will change the human experience. Perhaps then, matters that don't conform to our contemporary understanding of time, that is, things that haven't fit in with our conception of reality—that were considered bizarre or even crazy because of time constraints, such as time moving backward—may be regarded as plausible. Einstein-Rosen bridges like wormholes might be considered possible. Black holes could offer all kinds of opportunities to challenge our conception of time and how we live our lives."

Parker paused reflectively and then said, "But right now, Anna, when I truly think about it, I feel we're living in a dream world that's simply unreal."

Anna was silent for a moment and then said, "What you say is understandable, Parker. In some ways life *is* unreal. But we have to function in this *real* world if we're going to avoid problems." She paused momentarily, reflectively. "Have you experienced any incidents recently? You know, those unexplained dreams or visions that—"

"No," Parker said quickly. "As I said before, those things were of no significance. I suppose I do some daydreaming on occasion, like everybody." His brow knitted slightly reflecting some unease with the subject. Thoughts of Sarah flashed through his mind. For an instant he was inclined to mention his meetings with Sarah, but quickly dismissed the idea, worried that disclosure of the unusual encounters might provoke disturbing questions from the doctor.

"I sense some discomfort whenever we touch on these unexplained dreams and happenings," continued Anna, tapping her pencil slightly on a pad she was holding. "But we should talk about these things. As I've mentioned in previous sessions, it's important to control our emotions. Sometimes there can be a thin line between dreaming and actuality. People may imagine ghostly experiences that are quite real to them. In fact, some psychiatric studies have demonstrated strong connections between paranormal experiences and schizophrenia that—"

"But Anna, isn't that what I'm saying about time?" said Parker, interrupting. "Our life is unreal. It's an illusion."

Anna paused, looking down at her pad. "I understand, Parker. Now, I have some suggestions, some homework actually, that should help with your anxiety and depression."

Parker listened as the therapist discussed prescriptions and procedures, most of which he knew he would disregard. He sensed Anna's mind was elsewhere during his comments. Her expression, her careful glances at her watch. . . . As their session drew to a close he spoke carefully of depressive experiences that tended to trouble him, avoiding comments regarding his mother which could lead to protracted discussions that always left him uneasy. Although he could understand how the loss of his mother could lead to depression, it seemed improbable that it could cause him to imagine bizarre time-related events. According to Anna, wouldn't that make him schizophrenic? Just the thought increased his anxiety.

But he liked Anna. Although her appearance was right out of central casting for a psychologist (horn-rimmed glasses, boyish-bob haircut, stovepipe figure); Parker thought her attractive. But the more familiar he'd become with therapy, the less confidence he had. Indeed, he could find little clinical support for what he received from doctors for his money, beyond the pharmaceuticals. Yet, his psychiatric knowledge was limited at best, and didn't he always feel better after visiting Anna? He realized that she knew he had problems, yet she was careful, always supportive. But he had been cautious with Anna as well—discouraging any questions regarding the unexplained episodes in his life that occasionally surfaced. Events like time itself that defied reality. She might suspect a deeper, more advanced psychosis, but she never let on. And for that, he was grateful.

CHAPTER 22

It was an early evening in late October. Parker alighted from the Madison Avenue bus and walked west on 63rd Street toward his apartment on Fifth Avenue. A cool breeze came at intervals from Central Park, scattering autumn leaves that had collected amid wisps of debris in the gutter beside the road. A taxi rushed past suddenly and came to an abrupt stop halfway up the block ahead of him, its brake lights flashing in the darkness. As he drew close to the cab, a woman emerged, shot him the wary look he found typical of pedestrians on New York streets after dark, and quickly disappeared behind the safety of a doorway.

As he turned on to Fifth Avenue toward his apartment, the breeze picked up, and he drew the collar of his jacket tightly about his neck. At the entrance to his building, Robert the doorman greeted him with reserved dignity.

"Good evening, Mr. Livingstone," he said, opening the door.

"Hello, Robert," responded Parker. Offering a comment about the weather, he preceded the man into the building, where he acknowledged a restrained greeting from the two women at the front desk.

As he walked back toward the elevator, his thoughts turned again to Sarah. Since their recent meeting in the park when she had expressed her love for him he'd been able to think of little else. He'd become reconciled to the fact that she had been only a visitor to the penthouse—perhaps a relative or good friend of its residents. And he presumed she sometimes traveled to Europe. During one of their conversations she referred to "summer crossings," a quaint term his mother had used when referring to her trips to France and England.

There were no stops as he ascended in the elevator, but as he stepped from the car on his floor he was confronted by Mrs. Feddyplace emerging from her apartment. "Hello, Mrs. Feddyplace," he said moving toward the door to his unit. "It's nice to see you."

"What?" said the lady as she gained her bearings. "Oh, hello, Mr. Livingstone. I haven't seen you recently. Have you been away?"

"No, I've been here. Shall I keep the elevator for you?" he asked, stepping back and holding the door open to expedite the lady's departure.

"No, no, that's all right. I shall get it in a minute. Did you say you've been away?"

Reluctantly he let the door close, and with the passing of the elevator went hopes for a brief encounter. "No, I've been right here, ma'am. I see you're going down. Would you like me to push the button?" He turned toward the elevator.

"Oh, that's quite all right. I'm in no hurry. I'm having dinner downstairs in the dining room." There was an expectant lilt to her voice as though an invitation to dinner might be in the offing.

"I'm a bit late—meeting a friend tonight," he said quickly, preempting a possible invitation. "Here, let me get that elevator back for you." He pushed the button twice quickly, and then once more for good measure.

As he stood, trying to make small talk, it occurred to him that Mrs. Feddyplace, a longtime resident, might have some knowledge of the Thatchers or of Sarah. Given Sarah's age, she might not know her, but perhaps her family . . . or the Thatchers. . . . It wouldn't hurt to ask. Other efforts he'd made on social media had yielded nothing. Google alone had millions of hits or queries on the popular name "Sarah Holloway." And he was disinclined to approach the front desk after his recent experiences.

During a brief pause in their conversation he said, "By the way, Mrs. Feddyplace, would you happen to know the Thatchers or a person named Sarah Holloway? I believe Sarah may have been visiting in the pent—"

"Why, yes, of course," said the woman, brightening. "I've known Dolly Thatcher for years. She moved into the penthouse shortly after I came here. Lovely person. I haven't seen her in some time. She doesn't come out much anymore. She hasn't been well for a number of years—"

"Do you know Sarah Holloway?" Parker interrupted, eyeing the indicator of the returning elevator. "Miss Holloway was a young woman who may have been visiting the penthouse."

"No . . . no, I don't know the name," said the woman, inclining her head thoughtfully. "I don't think Dolly had visitors during recent years. Years ago she had a young lady who was her amanuensis. She was a rising star on the Broadway stage. Dreadful accident. She became stranded in the old elevator. Perished! But that was long ago. No one talks about it—oh, here's my car," said the lady, moving toward the opening door of the elevator. "It's nice to see you, Mr. Livingstone. Perhaps we can have tea some afternoon." The door closed on a smiling Mrs. Feddyplace, for an instant a glimmer of the pretty face that appeared at her cotillion years before.

Startled by the woman's comments, Parker stood staring at the closed door. Could he believe what Mrs. Feddyplace said? She was easily confused. But her reference to the old elevator was astonishing. His need for clarification exceeded all else. No longer concerned with the building's protocol or privacy issues, he knew his next step would be the front desk. Given their concern for security in the building, the ladies at the entrance would surely know Sarah.

Thoughts racing, he waited anxiously as the elevator reappeared, and then he descended to the main floor. As he approached the reception area one of the women who was standing at her desk hung up her phone, and glanced in his direction. "Hello, Mr. Livingstone," she said with a tight smile. "May I help you with something?"

"Evening, Miss Willoughby," he said. "I was looking for a young lady. I believe she may have been visiting someone in the penthouse."

The woman looked at him as though unsure what he'd said. "I beg your pardon?" she asked, her brow knitting slightly. "Are you referring to the Thatchers?"

"I'm not sure. It may have been the Thatchers," he said, adding uneasily, "Her name is Sarah Holloway. I believe she was a visitor in the penthouse."

The woman stared at him blankly; her colleague sitting at the desk behind her looked up abruptly. The two women exchanged glances briefly and the woman closest to him answered rather coolly, "I'm sorry, sir. We have no information regarding Thatcher guests." She turned slightly at her desk and picked up a slip of paper, indicating an end to their conversation.

Parker, feeling confused and rebuffed, hesitated, offered a quiet thank you, and moved toward the door. So be it, he thought, wryly. The privacy of residents was in good hands at 822 Fifth Avenue.

As he left the building the doorman, who had been standing inside, followed him through the entrance. "Will you need a taxi this evening, Mr. Livingstone?"

"No, I guess not, Robert." Annoyed and frustrated, Parker glanced back inside the building where the two women were peering in his direction. Turning abruptly to the doorman he said, "Robert, do you know Miss Holloway? Sarah Holloway?"

"No, sir. I just heard you talking to Miss Willoughby." He glanced uneasily over his shoulder toward the interior of the building. It was clear as he moved toward the street that the man was uncomfortable with the conversation.

Dazed, Parker crossed the avenue to the park. Once he was inside under the trees, the darkness closed in, adding to his bewilderment. At the bench, he dropped down, hunching forward, hands covering his face, tumbling thoughts striving for order.

What he'd heard was mystifying. Was he imagining things? Or perhaps he'd misconstrued what he'd heard from Mrs. Feddyplace. Her somewhat vague comment about someone stranded in the old elevator. . . . Or maybe she'd been confused. A rumor perhaps, or something she'd dreamed. . . .

And what about Anna? The dissociative disorders to which she sometimes carefully alluded crowded his mind, pressing for recognition. Disorganized behavior, delusions, hallucinations. . . . He tried desperately to suppress the thoughts, sensing the creeping chills of a panic attack.

But then once again came thoughts of Sarah and their extraordinary meeting of a few nights before. When first he'd seen her under the lamp light he'd been captivated. Her professed love for him that followed had exceeded his greatest expectations, leaving him in a state of ecstasy.

Her concerns for their different worlds and lifestyles, although understandable, could be overcome. Of course there would be adjustments. She was an Upper East Side girl, presumably from a milieu of debutantes and high society, whereas he was of relatively modest social standing. But this, he reasoned, would all be mollified by his limitless love and dedication.

His racing thoughts returned to Mrs. Feddyplace. What he'd just heard from the elderly lady was mystifying. Had he misunderstood her comments? Someone stranded in the elevator years ago? Had she said it was a guest of the Thatchers? He immediately thought of Sarah. A jarring thought. He was jumping to conclusions, of course. Mrs. Feddyplace's aging mind was an old trunk stuffed with addled memories. Slowly, instinctively, he pulled his cell phone from his pocket.

It was difficult to see in the darkness. In the distance, through a small opening in the foliage beyond the craggy ridge of Manhattan skyline, sailed a pale, slender rim of the lunar sphere, the only trace of light other than his cell phone. Absently, he Googled the words "Sarah Holloway Stranded Elevator," and began scrolling idly through the seemingly endless results. Suddenly, to his utter astonishment, the following words burst from the screen:

Sarah Holloway Rising Broadway Star
Dies in Elevator Mishap

Stupefied, with trembling fingers he continued his scanning, disbelieving the entries, attributing them to some type of weird coincidence. Could they refer to one of Sarah's relatives? Her grandmother . . . cousin. . . . Suddenly, speculation was crushed. Before him on the screen, flashed an article from the *New York Times* bearing the achromatic hue of a very old photograph. Standing in front of Broadway's Mark Hellinger Theatre— young, smiling, radiant—was Sarah.

Stunned, he tried desperately to refocus. What was happening? Was it another one of his fantasies? Was he sleeping? Just another dream from which he'd awaken? Was he losing his mind? Anna's admonitions flooded his thoughts. The thin line between illusion and reality. He'd convinced himself long ago that life was unreal. But he believed he had control of his senses. He was not schizophrenic. But, slowly came a creeping realization . . . a vague chilling fear that his love for Sarah could be leading him into a ghostly world from which there would be no return. Yet, he was powerless. His love for her transcended everything else.

He leaned back on the bench, consumed by thoughts of their most recent meeting. Her expression of love . . . the kiss. . . . All he longed for at the moment was to be in her arms, to hold her, to show his total devotion. His passion to spend the rest of his life with her overcame all other emotions, even though now he sensed a passage to madness.

And then, sounds . . . at first, indistinct and mysterious . . . followed by footsteps, barely audible, approaching from beyond the bend in the walk . . . closer, the confident tapping of heels tripping down the cobblestones. He straightened, listening intently. Was it possible? There was only one walk like that . . . the sauntering gait, the carefree swinging of the pocketbook. . . . Then, the cool immutable words from the darkness, "Hi, Parker. I'm back, Parker!"

— END —

ABOUT THE AUTHOR

Bernard F. Conners, former publisher of the *Paris Review*, has had a distinguished career in government, business, publishing, and film. He is the best-selling author of *Cruising with Kate, Dancehall, Tailspin, The Hampton Sister*s, and *Don't Embarrass the Bureau.* Mr. Conners lives in Loudonville, New York.

Page design and typesetting
Toelke Associates
Old Chatham, New York
www.toelkeassociates.com

Text composed in ITC New Baskerville
Chapter heads and numbers in Plaza D
Folios in Linotype Didot

Printed on 55# Glatfelter Natural
bound in Arrestox B Black Cloth

Printing and binding
Versa Press
East Peoria, Illinois
www.versapress.com